Seeking Thirst

By Carlene Sobrino Bonnivier

ISBN: 978-1501001321

Cover image: Melissa Nolledo
Book design: Future Studio Los Angeles

Carlene Sobrino Bonnivier
cbonnivi@gmail.com

Seeking Thirst

Seek ye thirst, and waters from
the very ground shall burst.
— Rumi

CARLENE SOBRINO BONNIVIER

CHAPTER ONE

Taking a Risk

Some would say it began before consciousness, before words, in the mists and shimmers before time. Others would say it began at seven o'clock behind the shed.

"Listen up, people. I don't want to have to tell you twice. You are inmates. This is a work crew but you are inmates, and you are doing time. Any goofing off, you go down to the Branch."

The policewoman is not quite five feet tall. Her hair is long, black and wavy. Her lips and her nails are fire engine red. There is enough equipment around her waist for anyone looking at her for the first time would not to see anything else for a while.

"If you're late for roll call once," she continues, "you wash the toilets. If you're late more than once, it's down to the Branch."

She likes this phrase, says it often and accompanies it with a slow but emphatic draw of her thumb through the air, like an underwater hitchhiker. Her eyes remain dry and sharp upon the work crew. If they miss one day, or if they smart off or don't do their work or…she relaxes her poster for a moment and smiles, nodding her head in rueful foreknowledge of the fate awaiting them should they ever cross her.

Carol, like many of the work crew, could remember very little about being arrested. She remembered driving down to Pacifica with Fran and Katie, meeting the other teachers at The Mediterranean. Did she eat? She'd been drinking martinis. Vaguely she remembered having gone from the restaurant to a bar, that most of the others had gone home. Who was she with? She more or less remembered leaving the bar and someone—either Fran or Katie—arguing with her. It was Katie. She didn't want Carol to drive. She refused to get into Carol's car. Blankness then until the red and blue lights in the rear view mirror. Stepping out of the car. She had recognized the particular view of the city that came lurching up to her as the police turned her around and handcuffed her. She was on Portola Drive, three or four blocks from home. She had driven thirty or forty miles in a blackout.

She remembered well asking the police to just let her stop and tell her husband what had happened, but they wouldn't, and they added that there'd be no phone call either till they thought she was sober enough. She went in and out of consciousness on the ride down to jail, though she had probably stayed awake the whole time. She was nearly sober by the time they took her photograph. Fully conscious by the time she went into the cell.

She stood just inside the bars, and then she leaned her back against them to steady herself. There were two women on the bunk beds to her right. They were asleep or passed out on yellow vinyl mattress, their faces to the wall. Dim yellow lights from the hallway cast a film upon the scene which was methodically washed by the flashing neon light coming through the narrow window near the ceiling. The light hit the women's feet, and Carol saw that they were black with dirt. Maybe it was from the floor. She brushed her foot across it. It was gritty but slippery, too.

There was a lidless toilet against one wall from which came the fulsome odor of Pine Sol and urine. Next to it was a water tap with an open pipe in the floor beneath it, no grate.

She wondered where she was. Maybe the Tenderloin. She had no idea where the city jail might be.

She hears a rattling of keys behind her. "Move it, honey." It is a policewoman, her keys in one hand and, in the other, three breakfast trays, stacked. She waits with a big sigh of impatience for Carol to move away from the door before she'll turn the key. As she enters the cell, she eyes Carol suspiciously. Does she think Carol's going to try to escape?

"You are nothing. Nothing at all." Carol hears the words, but the policewoman hasn't spoken, she is sure of it.

Carol shakes her head, to clear her head. "Can I call my husband now?"

The policewoman seems not to hear her, but after she puts the trays down on the floor, she straightens up, hands on hips, and says, "You need something to do, eat your breakfast." Then she points to a vacant cot. "Take a load off, honey." Carol sits down. "Take your shoes off, if you lay down. If you don't, I'll have to take them off you." Then something like a smile crosses the officer's lips. "Might as well get some sleep. You'll be here for awhile." She saunters out the door and locks it. Then she says,

"You'll make your call when we say you're ready."

Carol felt suddenly very tired. She slipped off her shoes and lay back on the vinyl mattress, not looking first, not wanting to know what might be on it. There was still too much alcohol in her, though, and the room started a slow spin. She sat up and leaned against the wall. It was cold, but that was all right. She waited. Soon the room stopped turning. Maybe she'd feel better if she ate. She reached over for one of the trays on the floor, and, as she did, she felt her stomach heave. She managed to bring the tray to her lap. Then she waited for her stomach to settle. She was covered in sweat, the dank medicinal smell of gin oozing through her pores. She wished she were at home. In the steam room. She wished she could call Frank.

Carol removed the lid from her tray and saw some scrambled eggs on a Styrofoam plate. Maybe it was the poor lighting, the confusion from the blinking neon, but it looked to her as though the eggs were nearly as white as the Styrofoam. There was also on the tray a piece of white bread and what had to be a slice of cheese encased in cellophane. She peeled the wrapper from the cheese and smelled it. It had no smell. She took a bite. It had no taste. It felt cold and slippery. She looked to see if maybe she'd left some of the plastic on it. She couldn't really tell. She tried the eggs. They tasted like lard and had the texture of mushrooms. She looked at the women, away from the eggs, and swallowed.

My God, she thought, as she took another bite, I could have killed someone. All these years of driving home with no memory of it—hundreds of times.

She stopped to try to figure out the numbers. She drank every day, but blacked out maybe only once a week. Fifty-two weeks. How many years? Twenty? Ten would be 520 times, so 1040. Over 1000 times, easily, and she had not killed anyone. Had she? There were never any dents in the cars. She'd looked. Over 1000 times she had awakened wondering where she was, what she'd done the night before, and then had gotten up and wondered where the car was, except for the few years she'd had a garage, and sometimes, even then, it wouldn't be there and she'd wondered how she got home, who took her, what had happened before that, where she had left the car, how she could find it. A few times she'd hunted for days and couldn't find it, so she reported it stolen and let the police find it. It was funny. It had always been funny.

Carol felt a knot in her stomach. She looked down at the tray. She'd eaten all of the eggs and the cheese and bread and even the cellophane.

Immediately she felt a knot tighten. It was about to spring loose. Carol rushed across to the toilet, and she could taste the lardy eggs and, from the night before, olives, pimientos and gin. Then she lost it all and was grateful to lose it all. She wished she could continue ridding herself of it and of every shameful time she had ended up on her knees in front of a toilet.

Her legs trembled as she turned the water tap on and rinsed her mouth and hands. She had crossed the floor in her stockinged feet. Now she rinsed her feet with her stockings still on them and then tip-toed back to her bunk, put the lid back on the tray and the tray back on top of the others, and removed her stockings. Then she just sat there holding her wet stockings in her hands.

"I could have killed someone," she said aloud this time. She looked again at the women across from her, and she thought that it could have been them. They could be dead lying there. She could have crashed into either one of them or she could have run them over in the street, and someone would be coming in here now to tell her she'd killed them and she wouldn't even know who they were. She wouldn't even remember hitting them. Or would their bodies have been like the red and blue lights, something to bring her back when it was already too late. Would she have a vision of them flying over the hood of her car? "Then what?" she asked herself. Would she stop drinking?

"Hey, who you talking to in there?" The policewoman entered the cell and picked up the trays. "You still drunk? Don't you want to make your phone call?"

"Yes, of course I do."

"Then of course you'd better stop talking to yourself." She took the trays and clanged the metal door behind her, turned and looked hard back into the cell.

"You something all right. You still awake. Them two is passed out. And you got the highest blood-alcohol level of the three of you: twenty-six."

"What do you need to prove I was drunk?"

The policewoman laughed. "We don't need but ten. I'd say that was one test you scored real high in."

"When can I make my call?"

"That's for me to know," she glanced down to her clipboard, "Carol. I'll let you know, Carol." Then she sauntered off.

Her name sounded like "Karo," the way the policewoman had just said it. Well, was it any worse, any more cloying, than "Carol?" She'd never liked her name. Never thought it suited her. Now here in this place, the syrupy way the woman had said it, made her think, as she had thought many times before, that she should change her name. Underlying that thought was the unstated hope that if she did change her name she would somehow change who she was. Years ago, when she married Frank, she had hoped that taking his name might do it. And she had tried to be whoever and whatever it was that he wanted her to be. Still she did not feel changed. She felt hidden.

She had tried to talk this over with him once, early in their marriage. They were eating dinner. He seemed relaxed. She began with the desire to change her name, not the deeper thing because she wasn't sure of it or how to say it, and he wanted always to know the point and from that point they could discuss something.

So she began, "I've been thinking of changing my name."

He laughed and said, "You want to be a star or something?"

She pretended to share his amusement. "A whole constellation, I think."

"Really," he said, "is there something on your mind?"

"No," she had said, but she wondered to herself, 'Wasn't changing my name something on m mind?' She retreated. "How's the roast?"

"Great. Just the way I like it. Pink in the middle."

Carol had become a good cook. Her first job had been as a waitress, and she'd always been interested in the ways different groups of people cooked and what they chose to eat. For a period of time she'd played with the idea that she could discover her heritage by identifying what kind of food she was just naturally drawn to, but her taste seemed to change with her mood, so this idea soon joined all the other wild attempts she'd made at self discovery: they slipped into the most arid regions of her imagination, beckoning, never paying off.

It wasn't so bad, really, being married to Frank. He preferred meat and potatoes, but he would try, once a week or so, to eat something different, an Indian curry or something Mexican. He didn't mind the spices, but just not too often.

*   *   *   *   *

The next day at school, as she moved from one student to the next, guiding their hands as they held their brushes or helping them adjust the intensity of their colors, she found herself thinking about the short exchange she'd had with Frank. She'd learned something: she liked the idea of a constellation. It brought an image to her of bright beauty, elegant and mysterious. It had a feeling to it of connection but still a wild sort of freedom. The sense, too, of destiny, of an actual plan. Lights and configuration, a way to shore or to a sea more familiar.

During her first free period she went into the school library and found that there were actually eighty-eight constellations. She'd had no idea there were so many. Of course she knew there were trillions of anonymous stars in the night sky, but it amazed her that so many had configured in human eyes and were named. The scientists looking through their telescopes or the poets looking into a clear night sky—they saw so much more than she did with her paints and her canvas. She wanted to see more. She would be her own constellation. Now she was thrilled, full of herself, really, and sure that today, right now, she was going to find her name.

As she turned the pages in the astronomy book, she said the names of the constellations out loud, quietly, but loudly enough for her to feel the words on her lips. "Carol" had always required a smile. She wanted a name that she could say without smiling, yet she wanted something open and easy. About two-thirds of the way through the listings she saw it: Orion. She said it out loud: Orion. That was it. She closed the book.

"Devon, Carol." It was the policewoman again. "Time to make your phone call."

*   *   *   *   *

Frank was there to get her before seven. The look on his face. He was pale, sick with worry. No anger, never any anger. This was as bad as she'd ever been, and she'd never been in jail before. Still, no anger. Disappointment. Silence. A cross he bore not on his back, but before him, like a shield.

On this early and very ugly Saturday morning, as they drove home, she was numb with shame and nearly grateful for the silence. She did tell him what she could remember of the night before, and he told her what he'd done, the hospitals and the one friend—Katie—that he'd called, how worried he had been. How worried her friend was, and she'd better call Katie when she got home. She could see it was true that he had been worried. It was on his face, and she was grateful that he cared about her, at least in this way. They drove the rest of the way home in silence.

"I'm sorry I can't stay with you," he said, dropping her off in front of their house. "You know the guys'll be counting on me. It's too late to get another fourth. I'm really sorry."

"Thanks. I'm okay. I'm very sorry I worried you so much. You're going to be tired for the game."

"You know me. I'll pull in my reserves."

Carol ventured a smile. Frank patted her on the head as he shook his own. "Get some sleep."

She stood at the front door, looking at the electronic key-pad that would disengage the alarm and allow her to enter her home. For a moment she couldn't remember the combination, but when she lifted her hand, her fingers automatically hit the right buttons.

Home, a place she had loved dearly a year ago when they first moved to San Francisco from Sacramento. The house was made of Redwood, 50's modern, built solidly into a hillside west of Noe Valley. They had a good view of the bay. She had loved the house because it was beautiful, but also because, like anything new, it held possibility.

They worked on the house. Painted the walls the colors she'd chosen, a wheat color with accents in smaller areas of deep blue. They worked in silence painting, refinishing, decorating. There were lots of windows, double paned against the winds that swept across the hillside, double paned against the damp summer fog. When the day was bright and she felt the tension go out of her body, the hope arose in her that maybe on this day she could turn to him and he would not turn away and they would manage to say something of what was on their minds or in their hearts. She remembered, wryly, those were usually the days he put down the paintbrush or the sandpaper, picked up his clubs or his racket, and went out to play. Sometimes it was a relief to her. She felt less lonely when he was gone.

Carol was sentenced to forty-eight hours in jail with the option of serving that time on a work crew on Saturdays and Sundays for three weekends. She chose the work crew and then, surprising herself, chose the public golf course her husband played nearly every Saturday. "Pacific Pines," she said, and had to stop herself from smiling.

* * * * *

"Devon! Carol Devon!"

"Yes. Here."

"Look alive there, Devon. You ain't been drinking this morning now have you?"

"No. Sorry. I was thinking of something."

"Yeah, well don't think too much, Devon. We want you to work while you're here. No time to daydream. Get it?"

"Yes."

"Good." The policewoman then addressed the crew at large and the newcomers in particular. "Pick up a vest and put it on so we can find you anytime we want to. Don't take it off till it's time to go home." She looked again at Carol and said, "Pick up one of them rakes and go with that inmate over there." She pointed to a blonde woman standing next to one of the three-wheeled Cushmans lined up against the shed.

The policewoman continued to address the work crew as they put on the bright orange vests that identified them as inmates. "You can go where you want on the course. Rake up the leaves and pick up the trash like I said." She turned her attention to a man wearing a baseball cap, and she smiled. "Now some of you guys like to have competitions to see who can find the most golf balls, and that's fine." Then she looked over to a few of the men who didn't seem to be paying close enough attention. "But you stay out of the water and stay out of the way of the golfers. Be sure and don't bother them." Then back to the group at large. "Don't stop to get coffee or nothing at the Club House. That's for the golfers, and they don't like eating with criminals. You get back here to the shed for roll call at lunchtime. You can come back for the break if you want to." Then she added, reluctantly, Carol thought, "We'll have coffee and doughnuts."

"Doughnuts," Carol said aloud and then caught herself. She was a criminal now. She could eat doughnuts. She was smiling when she reached the figure by the cart that was waiting for her with her eyes fully upon her. The look surprised Carol. The man with the baseball cap said something to her and the other woman about taking good care of the vehicle. He was apparently in charge though he wore an orange vest like theirs.

"Come on. Let's go." The woman jumped into the driver's seat and started the engine. Carol got into the passenger side, and they took off straight up a hill. The steep grade frightened Carol slightly, but she said nothing and concentrated on the grove of pine trees ahead of them. The morning fog lay heavy in the trees, the ones closest dark green and misty blue, the ones in the distance nearly black. When they reached the trees, the scent of pine filled Carol's lungs, and she felt very different— light, exhilarated.

They continued up through the grove until it became too dense to maneuver easily. The woman stopped the engine, got out and motioned Carol to follow her. They walked to the top of the hill and then turned along the ridge and went down a few feet.

"Where are we?" Carol felt a slight apprehension.

"Between the golf course and the shooting range." The woman sensed Carol's uneasiness. "Don't worry," she said smiling again, and Carol noted that she had beautiful straight white teeth and that her eyes were blue. "I know it's your first day, so I just wanted to show you that it's not going to be that bad. Come on."

"And the shooting range?"

The woman smiled again. "Too early for them. They don't start till ten on weekends."

She led Carol over to a row of eucalyptus. Then she stood very still and whispered, "Look over there. It's a jack rabbit prairie."

Carol looked and saw the jackrabbits standing stock-still on an open plain just beyond the trees. The rabbits, standing on their hind legs, looked like miniature kangaroos. For a second they didn't look real. Then one of the rabbits hopped forward while a second one took a hop or two off to the side. Almost immediately they came to an abrupt halt, the other rabbits having moved not a bit. The women waited another minute, and two more rabbits, in tandem, disengaged themselves from the tapestry, took a few hops off in one direction or another, and then, like the two that had gone before them, froze back into the still, quiet scene.

"When they're standing still," Carol's companion whispered, "you could doubt they'd ever moved."

"I can't figure out what the purpose is. Why they're doing that."

Carol laughed, loudly. The rabbits turned, as one, in her direction, and it made her laugh more to be discovered and, as it appeared to her from their unblinking eyes, accused. When the women got back to the Cushman, Carol said, "I think that's the first time I've laughed since I got arrested."

"You didn't laugh then, I hope."

"Oh God no! That really wasn't funny."

"No," the woman said more soberly, "that wasn't funny for me, either." When her companion started up the cart, Carol noticed how strong her arms and hands were. And the color of her skin. A light gold, like wheat.

"What's your name?"

"Brigid. Yours is, 'Devon, Carol!'"

Surprising herself, Carol said, "Orion. Please call me Orion."

"Spelled like the one with the belt?" Orion nodded. "That's beautiful."

Orion was pleased with herself, pleased that she had said her name, pleased with Brigid. This wasn't going to be bad at all.

Within an hour the two women were sweating as they raked and bagged leaves and picked up whatever the golfers had left behind: wrappings, mostly from cigarette packs and candy bars; sometimes scorecards, aluminum cans, half-pints of whiskey. Did the booze loosen them up or make their game worse? Orion wondered. She wished she could see her own behavior when she was in a blackout. She wondered if her words slurred or even made sense or if she was, as she was often told, deep and perceptive and self-assured. She could hardly imagine it. She could imagine the other times, at home with Frank, when she suffered bouts of self-pity and anguish. If pressed, he would tell her what happened the night before, but with only the briefest and faintest indication of how she appeared or what she'd said. She got, mostly, silence in which her imagination would, one moment, pull back, saying it couldn't have been too bad, and in the next moment, rush forward with possibilities so garish and humiliating she could feel her face burn.

"What are you thinking about?"

Orion smiled. "I was wondering what I'm like when I'm drunk."

"You don't remember?"

"Do you?"

"Well, I'm sure I don't remember it in quite the same way someone else would, but, yes, I remember. I've never had a blackout. I know everyone here says it, but I really don't drink very often and I don't usually drink a lot. I did that night—the night I was arrested—and I have on other occasions, but few and far. I don't think I've ever had a blackout, but then again I guess if I did I wouldn't remember, would I?"

Orion laughed. "Well, no, but you might remember that there's an hour or two of the night before that you can't account for or you don't know how you got home or where your car is or any number of things."

"It must be an awful feeling to wake up with."

"Yes," Orion said, looking clearly into Brigid's blue eyes, "it's a terrible feeling," and then she had an odd and sudden urge: She wanted to take Brigid's hands in hers. She didn't, of course.

"When I wake up I have such a feeling of...." Orion searched for the right word, the honest word, not quite believing she could possibly be saying these things out loud. "It's a feeling of dread. Like I'm doomed. And I feel utterly alone."

"Why don't you stop drinking—or have you tried?"

"I haven't really tried. Since I was arrested I've been more aware of how much I'm drinking and I don't drink and drive, but otherwise...."

"You think you need a better reason?"

"Yeah."

"You wouldn't just do it for yourself?"

Orion laughed. "No."

"Guess I'm pretty egotistical. I do everything for myself, just for me."

"You don't seem egotistical. I mean you seem very warm, interested."

Brigid smiled. "Well, I guess I am right now."

The two women looked at each other for a moment and then Orion became very self-conscious, turned, picked up a rake and went back to work. They worked and talked for the rest of the morning. Brigid was a carpenter, active in the politics of getting women into the carpenters' union and into jobs. Orion said, "I am an artist," and then she added that she taught part time at a high school. Always before she had said, "I'm an art teacher." Always before she had first said that she was married.

"I admire your courage," Brigid said. "I'm a sculptor, myself, but I don't find much time for it. Just whenever I take a vacation. Or sometimes on weekends. Of course, this has definitely put an end to that for awhile."

Orion knew that Brigid was assuming she had given up the money or the security of a full-time job for the uncertainties of a life devoted to art. She knew she should tell her she was not courageous at all, that she was married and well taken care of and that her husband and everybody else thought of her teaching and her art work as hobbies. But she was too ashamed to say any of this; and there was something about this reality, this hard physical work and speaking from the heart, that made her feel disconnected from her life with Frank.

The women worked and talked the whole morning,

forgetting the coffee and doughnuts. It was nearly noon when Brigid said, "We've got to get back in time for roll call or it'll be 'down to the Branch.'"

After roll call the inmates filed past the brown bags lined up on a table near the entrance to the shed. By now there was a glimmer of sunshine, but most everyone went inside and sat down. There was music on the radio and, Orion sensed, a feeling of camaraderie that was drawing everyone in. The two women joined one of the tables, and Orion took out her sandwich and looked to see what was in it.

The man who'd signed their cart out to them, whom everyone called Captain Cushman, pointed across the table to Carol saying, "That bread's made in Folsom Prison and sent to you fresh once a week."

Another man said, "Fresh?"

And a woman said, "Yeah, well that lunchmeat's not made in Heaven either," and they all smiled. Orion felt wonderful sitting there with the other inmates, eating stale bread and greasy lunchmeat. And she'd had a good workout that morning. She felt strong, very pleased with herself.

She looked across at Brigid. "I think it's going to be okay here." Brigid flashed her great smile and nodded, and they all continued talking, telling each other anything at all. It was the intimacy of strangers, Orion thought. I can talk and they can talk because we know we'll probably never see each other again. She said this later to Brigid.

"Yeah, I think it's that. But it's something else, too. I mean how many pretensions can you have when everyone here knows you were drunk and no doubt making a big fool of yourself. And we were all treated to the same humiliations in jail. It's a real leveler, getting arrested and put in jail. A leveler, kind of like death."

"And have we all gone to heaven, then?"

"You really do like it here, don't you?"

"It's funny, but I do."

By afternoon the sun was shining, and the women were working with Captain Cushman and a woman named Mary, who was really a mess. She was only 21 years old, but she had hardly any teeth and couldn't have weighed more than 80 pounds. She was a black woman and had hair so thick and wild that it looked like a Halloween wig. Mary never took a break, never sat or even stood still for a second. She just worked like a fury.

"How can she keep that up?" Orion asked.

"I've wondered that myself," Brigid said. "She is always like that, too. And they've tested her for drugs. She's clean. It seems like just some terrible compulsion. She can't stop doing whatever she's doing. It made her late for roll call once since I've been coming here, so she's already had toilet duty. We all try to watch out for her and make sure she gets back in time."

"How much more time do you have here?"

"One more weekend."

"Oh."

"Do you live in the city?"

"Yeah," she said and then, very deliberately, "We have a place in Noe Valley."

"'We'?"

"I'm married. My husband and I." Orion thought she caught a slight shaking of Brigid's head, a slight regret of some sort. "Is anything wrong?"

Brigid smiled, but was definitely shaking her head, "No. Not at all. You just don't seem married. You certainly didn't mention it before."

Orion knew that it was true, and she started to apologize, but that didn't seem appropriate either, so she just stood there silent and uncertain.

Captain Cushman came over and said, "It looks to me like you're ready for a break, ladies, and I'm dying for a chili dog with lots of cheese and onions. What do you say?"

"Are you going to the Club House?" Brigid asked.

"Yeah. Come on."

Orion took a step back and halted, frightened that she might see Frank, wondering if she was really ready to have Frank see her in a bright orange vest and with these people. Captain Cushman noticed the worried look on Orion's face.

It'll be all right. I'm an old-timer here. I've already done eight of these weekends and I have another four weekends to go. Besides I'm a Captain and she," he drew his thumb through the air, indicating the direction of the shed, "is only a lowly lieutenant. Nobody's going to do anything to you."

"We'll just get the stuff to go," Brigid added. "Okay?"

Orion hesitated for a moment and then heard herself say in a very strong voice, "Yeah. Good. Let's go," and she felt, for the first time in years, the pleasure of taking a risk without first taking a drink.

CHAPTER TWO

Chaos Out of Order

C arol was twelve when she started working on West Temple at the Harmony House Cafe. She'd passed it hundreds of times on her way to Echo Park. Then she'd filtered into the place the way most of the neighborhood kids did at one time or another. They'd drink malts or cherry cokes or smoke cigarettes and drink black coffee, sometimes have a burger or French fries, mostly just hang out.

She had lied and said she was sixteen. Possibly she was fooling someone, but it wasn't the man who hired her. Mario had owned the Harmony House for years, back when the neighborhood had been Italian and Irish and Jewish. He used to talk about those days, mostly because he'd been a semi-professional boxer and so had some of the other men from the neighborhood. He had kept the fliers announcing their fights, and he had them framed and hanging from the walls of the Café. He himself would demonstrate his killer left-right combination, and he took the time to show it to Carol. He told her she was very good for a girl. She took that as a compliment, and she practiced her left-right combination and her footwork in the kitchen when business was slow.

When Mario still owned the place, he had told her that pots wouldn't cook the food evenly if they weren't uniformly clean inside and out. A good scrubbing of the pots, he added, made your biceps stronger, too, and that would quicken your left-right combination. They'd never see it coming. It was the same, he said, with a person's health. You had to stay healthy and eat good food if you wanted to be ready for a fight, and even though he cooked the burgers himself, he never ate them or the hot dogs and she never saw him drink a coke, either. He did drink thick black coffee and always smelled of cigars, but he never smoked them in the restaurant.

"Well," he said, "I'm old already. But now I know what I know and I'm telling you, it's not good just looking cute, Carol. You have to take care of yourself and eat healthy." Carol's concession to all of that was to not smoke in front of him. Sometimes she'd try to eat right, too.

Mario told Carol he thought she might be Italian, like him, at least part, because she had an olive complexion and thick black hair (though it was kinky enough, maybe she had some colored blood, but neither of them said it). Carol also had thick black eyelashes. "Be careful," he said, "who you look at sweetly with those eyes. Those lashes could hurt a man!"

Carol worked for Mario for just a few months before he sold the restaurant to two young white men, brothers. The older brother, Bill, was nice enough. Tall and slow talking. The younger one, Howard, was short and good-looking with curly hair and quick brown eyes. He had an ulcer and was mean to anyone he could be mean to. He knew

how to charm the customers, though, and when they asked about his health or his business or anything at all to do with him, he'd say it was excellent, really excellent.

Carol liked working for Bill. He would show her how to do things, and when she made mistakes he'd help her correct them. He'd shown her that there were systems to things and that organization was ninety percent of the job. She liked that. He'd shown her that even washing dishes provided an opportunity to create a system. She soaked all the knives and forks and spoons in scalding hot water. Then she soaped all the glasses and cups and dishes without disturbing the utensils. Then she took the utensils up one by one and scoured them. After that she put the pots and pans into the deep soapy water and, while they soaked, she rinsed the things she'd washed in the other sink, again using scalding hot water. With rubber gloves on, her hands could take it, and, after a while, she didn't need the gloves anymore.

She had developed her own system for stacking dishes, the big platters furthest away, then the dinner plates and saucers. The remaining area she filled in with glasses, cups, and bowls. The silverware she stacked with the tips up in the air to dry nicely. Then she scrubbed the pots and pans, the bottoms, too.

Neither Howard nor Bill seemed to notice how shiny, nearly spotless, she got the cookware. They didn't seem to be aware of her lashes, either, or even that she was a girl or that she probably wasn't sixteen. Except for those times that Bill was showing her how to do something, they didn't talk to her much. Howard, now and then yelled at her about not wasting so much butter on the toast or buttering the toast faster or not slicing the tomatoes so thick or slicing them faster. He often threatened to fire her. In front of the customers, he tried not to do anything unpleasant, but she had some faults that he could not refrain from commenting on. Her grammar, for example.

Once when he'd taken her into the back just outside the view of the customers he'd told her she'd "better get the lead out" and not be so slow getting to the toast when it popped up cause it got cold and then it was hard to spread the butter and that was why she was using up so much butter and that was why it took her so long to butter it.

Carol brushed passed him saying, "I don't have time to listen right now, and anyway I can't go more faster and do a good job." She was already in view of the customers when he yelled from the back, "'I can't go <u>any</u> faster,' you nitwit."

Carol stopped dead in her tracks, nothing smart to say back, the customers all heads up looking at her. She felt tears in her eyes. She blinked them both back and started to go on with her work. Howard came rushing out then, a big smile on his face. He pretended not to notice the customers, but just went straight over to her and patted her on the back saying, "Sorry, dear. I didn't mean to yell. Just want to help you learn." And then what did she do? She smiled back, part of the pretense. She didn't know why, exactly, but maybe it would raise her in the eyes of the customers. Maybe it just felt good to be talked to that way, even if it was all a show.

Once Howard shared an insight with her that forever put into her conscious mind the secret to dealing with people who were mean with the power they had over her. She'd done it, really, all her life. But she didn't know it till Howard helped her see it.

There was an old man who came almost every day, and he always had half a grapefruit for desert. Howard didn't like to bother with the tedious task of cutting into each individual section of the fruit, "moving the flesh away from the membrane," as he would say, so he gave the task to Carol. She was amazed by the shape of the grapefruit knife, and enjoyed learning how to use it. She was slow, of course, perfecting her method, and this irritated Howard. Now the old man was living on Social Security, and he was careful with his money. Maybe it was for that reason that he didn't leave tips, but Carol hadn't noticed it. She was too young or too inexperienced in the world of business to understand the return people looked for in an investment. One day when she was carefully and ever so slowly cutting perfect wedges into the old man's grapefruit, Howard said, "Don't bother, Carol, he'll never leave you a tip." Either he was trying to give her some business advice, Carol figured, or he was trying to be mean, letting her know once again she was a nitwit. Carol suspected it was both, that even when he was being nice he was being mean. She didn't know the word sabotage, but it was then that the insight came to her: 'Every time he tries to make me hurry up,' she vowed, 'I will just slow down slower.'

Mario had taken all his pictures and fliers down, and there were dim squares of white on the wall where the years of grilled onions and burgers had not quite penetrated. They were sad little squares to Carol. It felt like not just Mario was gone but the whole neighborhood that he'd talked about so proudly, it was gone, too. So it was a relief when the brothers painted the walls. Carol liked the soft colors they used, too. It seemed peaceful. They washed the big glass window in front, and they had hired an artist to paint "Harmony House Cafe" across the gleaming surface. Really, it looked sharp. The whole restaurant did. By the time they finished, it didn't look like anyone had ever eaten there before.

Then they went about ridding themselves of the kids, making them leave as soon as they finished eating, asking them to smoke outside. And they changed the menu. They made tuna salad with celery and sometimes with raisins or nuts. Once a week they put the tuna in a tomato they'd cut and spread open like a starfish. The burgers weren't the same, either. The meat was expensive, and if you wanted, you could order it rare. No hot dogs at all. Prices went way up.

Even though Carol didn't like Howard, Bill was nice enough and so she asked to stay on. She needed the money, but besides that, she knew she would be learning something.

The people who started coming in to the Cafe were different. They were white people from the offices that lay just beyond the neighborhood, farther into the heart of downtown Los Angeles. They all lived somewhere else. At the beach or in the valley, some places Carol had never heard of before, even though they said they were right there in Los Angeles. Mario still dropped in now and then, and he told Carol he was thinking of working at the Home where she lived. They always needed cooks and, he said, he missed the kids. That surprised Carol. As far as she was concerned, they were just kids who came and went and had nothing to do with her. Some, like her, were more or less permanent residents, but any of them, including her, could be gone in a minute.

September came, and when school started Carol couldn't wait lunches anymore. She was stuck with dinners, much slower, not as interesting as lunchtime, and there weren't as many tips. It was easier to get something good to eat at lunchtime too, as it was usually too busy for Howard to watch her every move, but at dinner he rarely missed. It confused Carol sometimes because she didn't always know what he would consider okay for her to eat, and if he said anything to her about it, she would burn with shame and anger. It was easier not to even try eating there when Howard was working, but just to get back to the Home for what remained of dinner.

The Junipero Serra Home wasn't part of the church or the school. In fact, she was the only kid in the Home who was also going to the Catholic school next door. The Home had all kinds of kids, not quite juvenile delinquents, but in trouble somehow and all under sixteen. Some, like Carol, were youngsters whose foster parents had given them up and placed them there; others had parents, but the Courts had taken them away for one reason or another and had not placed them with foster parents.

Serra wasn't a dingy place, but it had the feel to it of a bunker. It was built on the slant of a hill, and the school next door had filled in the sloping lot that lay between the two buildings. Then they paved over that land and straight onto the roof of the Home, and made the whole area a playground. If you happened to be in your room during recess or lunch time you could feel the thumps through the walls coming down through the ceiling, as the children ran and bounced balls above.

They bricked up all the windows in the wall on the side that was filled in, and there weren't many kids who wanted to stay in those dark rooms, though there were some. Usually, they placed the newcomers there.

On the other side of the building there were windows and Carol had been at the Home long enough to have maneuvered herself into a room with a window on the second floor. There were no bars on the second story windows, so, in addition to light, she had a means of escape when the front door was locked at night or anytime she wanted to avoid people downstairs. About a foot and a half away from the window casement, there was a fire ladder suspended from some hooks. Holding onto the window frame, Carol could just get her right foot onto a rung. Then, shifting her weight to her right foot and clinging to the casement with her left hand, she would stretch out her right arm and grab hold of the ladder. Then came a moment of steadying herself and gradually shifting of all her weight onto the right side. Then, she would grab the ladder with both hands, find a place for her left foot somewhere beneath the right one and start her way down.

She had to be careful not to pinch her hands between the ladder and the wall with the weight of her own body, and she had to be careful when she reached the bottom rung, as it stopped about eight feet from the ground. If she had the time, she'd swing over to the bars covering the window on the first floor and let herself down slowly. If she didn't have time, she jumped.

Carol loved having her own room. She kept it very clean and uncluttered. It surprised people—the few people she ever let into her room—when they saw how tidy it was. They expected something wild, but found a place as calm and orderly as a nun's cell. And it might have been, she spent so much time there alone, quiet and private, making her sketches, then hiding them away or balling them up and throwing them out, never showing them to anyone. And the other girls heard her practicing her footwork, boxing. She was really strange. If they were invited in, all they saw of her art work was the sharpened black pencils she kept tips up in a brown coffee mug and the clean thick paper she kept ready thumb-tacked to a board on her desk for the moment she needed it.

No one at the Home minded that she was late for dinner, as only breakfast was mandatory. On this particular night, Howard had kept her at work. He'd caught her smoking in the kitchen within view of a customer.

"Carol, this is the last time I'm going to let you get away with it. Next time I'm going to tell Bill, and he has already talked to me about some of the stunts you pull."

Carol didn't say anything, but if he could read eyes at all, Howard would know she didn't believe him.

"If he wants to fire you, I can't stop him, you know. Now why don't you wash the floor up where you were flicking the ashes, and you might as well do the rest of it while you're at it."

"Is this punishment?"

"Let's say, it'll help me forget to tell Bill."

Carol never admitted it when she was wrong, but she understood very clearly that there were consequences to her behavior, and she took some pleasure in accepting those consequences, often punishing herself before anyone else had the chance to. There had been times when, for one reason or another, she had taken the blame for something she hadn't done. That was different. She didn't know exactly why she did that, but it had something to do with proving she could deal with life's injustices. This little punishment, washing a floor, was easy enough. So was going without dinner.

By the time she'd finished the floor, all the customers had gone. Howard was pretending that he wasn't waiting for her to finish, but he'd already thrown his apron into the laundry and turned on the night-lights. He was standing behind the counter, polishing it for what Carol thought was probably the hundredth time, when she gathered her things together and walked past him to the front door of the Cafe. There she paused, took out a cigarette, lit it, and blew a triple-smoke-ring farewell to Howard before she walked out the door.

It was only three blocks from the Harmony House to the Home, but the neighborhood changed quickly once you left Temple Street and headed toward the church. Carol was feeling good smoking her cigarette after the hard work she'd done, so she walked the three blocks slowly, liking the twilight on the flowers and the sun and shadow on the small neat squares of grass in front of the houses.

Whenever she was peaceful enough to think about it, walking those blocks home, she would wonder about the families that lived in the houses along the way. It was mostly old people now. Old people who had time for flowers and yards. They were probably already too old to move away when the rest did or else they wanted to live near the church. "I wouldn't stay here for anything," she said out loud, but she looked with some envy at the bushes full of lilac flowers and the ground turned up beneath them, at the climbing flowers that looked like they were made of paper, covering the trellises and parts of stucco walls. The walls seemed soft and warm with the slanting gold and red of the setting sun. She would sketch the walls and the paper flowers when she got back to the Home.

Carol was just going into her room when she heard Denise. "Hey, Carol, come over here." She went over. "Look what I got." Denise held out a plastic bag. "It's Acapulco Gold. My brother got it for me in T.J."

"Oh. When did you see your brother? I thought he was gone somewhere."

"Texas. I told you, Texas. Well, he's back. He had a ball. Sneaked across the border with this great stuff. He told me all about it. Said maybe next time he'd take me with him."

"Great. Have a good time."

"Oh, Carol, I'm not going right this minute. Just sometime when he goes, he's going to take me."

"Okay. Well, if you haven't left before I get back, maybe you could roll a few joints and we'll play cards or something."

"Okay. I'll just wait in your room."

"You know I don't like anyone to be in my room when I'm not there."

"I'll just roll the joints there, then I won't have to go back and forth and get the papers and everything."

"Well, don't touch anything. Okay?"

"I never do. I never touch anything."

Carol gave Denise a hard look, but then she nodded an okay and went down the stairs to the dining hall.

There was still some food left from dinner. Carol got a tray and pushed it along the stainless steel rails, rubbing the steamy glass panes with her fist, trying to see what there might be to eat. Vegetable soup, greasy. Mashed potatoes. She got three scoops with butter, extra butter to spread across the memory of Howard's stinginess. A dish of tomatoes. A slice of lemon. No string beans, too soggy, too greasy.

Suddenly Carol was aware of someone watching her. She lifted her eyes and saw a friendly face smiling at her from across the counter.

"Mario!" Carol ran down to the cashier's station and around

back, behind the counter. The old man met her and they embraced. The sweet familiar odor of cigars seemed to open something in Carol's heart. She felt tears in her eyes. Abruptly, she moved away from the old man, a huge smile on her face.

"Mario. It's great you're here. When did you start?"

"Just today. Just now. I'll be working mostly dinners. I've been looking for you. You're really late tonight."

"Oh, some extra work at the Harmony. Howard."

"He's something, but you can handle him, Carol."

"Maybe."

"Hey, I saved you some roast beef, medium rare. Maybe more medium by now."

"Oh, that's so nice. Thank you."

Mario went back into the kitchen and Carol returned with her tray, parking herself in front of the door while she waited for him.

"Here you are." He presented her with a platter and arranged the food that she'd already taken around the beef, added a small piece of parsley. "Eat the parsley, Carol. It's good for you."

"I will. Gee, it's great you're here, Mario."

"Good," he said. "I'm glad you are glad."

They chatted for a few minutes. Then Mario excused himself. He had to help close down the kitchen for the night. "But I'll see you tomorrow," he said, and Carol felt like replying with something bold like 'Thank God,' but she just nodded and smiled.

The hall was still full of girls talking and laughing, a few studying. It was the eating hall, the study hall, the day room, the night room, and, sometimes, the recreation room and sometimes the theater. It was the only place the girls could socialize.

Now and then they could have boys over, but very few of the girls were willing to put their potential boyfriends through the discomfort of being watched by every other girl in the room.

Carol didn't spend much time with any of the other girls. Now and then someone would come through that she thought was interesting, but they were usually the girls who only stayed for a few days till their parents came for them. Denise was her only friend at the Home, and she was her friend only because it didn't seem to matter how rude Carol was to her or how much she discouraged her. Denise persisted. Carol allowed.

When Carol got back to her room, Denise was waiting for her, lying down on Carol's bed with her shoes on, right on Carol's bedspread.

"Feet!"

Denise swung them onto the floor and sat up. "You're so fussy. You're worse than the nuns."

"You're a slob."

"Does that mean my stash isn't good enough for you?"

"I'll bet you haven't rolled any joints. I'll bet you haven't even cleaned the grass, have you?"

"What of it?"

"Where is it?"

Denise threw the plastic bag across to Carol who had seated herself as far away from Denise as she could.

"You know I made that bedspread myself."

"How could I forget?"

Carol began to separate the slender dry leaves from the twigs and the seeds. She was sorry she had let Denise come with her the night they'd gone to Lillie's work and stolen the material for the bedspread and for the curtains that now hung primly on

Carol's windows. She was happy with what she had made, but she was sure she'd made a big mistake letting Denise come. She had a big mouth. Sooner or later Denise would tell.

Carol lit the joint she had rolled. It was tight and smooth and nearly perfect. She inhaled deeply and held the smoke down as she passed the cigarette on to Denise.

The black and white rectangles of the heavy cotton that draped the windows fell neatly into rows. They fell like so much clarity might fall, black and white, yes and no, up or down or across, neat fields of order.

*   *   *   *   *

The mountains stacked up one behind the other in broad low swatches. Orion was looking west from the Pacific Crest Trail which ran all the way from Canada to Mexico. She was near the Oregon border, in the Marble Mountain Wilderness. The Trinity Alps lay to the South. It was August, but they were still covered with snow. Looking west, though, to the closest range, the mountains were full of sweet and sorrowful colors, lilac, indigo, blue. Orion concentrated, trying to name the colors of the trees, trying to see beauty that she knew she had seen before. Nearest her were the green pine and spruce, going dark green, giving way to blue then purple, and then a lighter misty blue, out until there was only sky to carry the color. It was a silky sky she could wrap herself in, she could sigh and dissolve into, lose herself.

She was supposed to be finding herself, the safety of these solid mountains giving her strength to cross the desert again, no hope for facts, desperate hope for honesty. Could she be honest? Beauty could help her. It had always helped her. But when she looked, she saw jagged fragments and chaos, gashes and chasms. The only clear image that came to her was a series of bombed out bridges.

The mind, someone said, could take you only as far as despair. That was where it had taken her all right. She couldn't think anymore, she knew that, but now she hardly had the strength to want anything but despair. Her senses, her sense of beauty, that was all she could think of that might push her into some other state of being. She tried to see with her eyes the beauty she had seen almost always before, before she had picked up the phone and called Brigid and ruined her life.

"God, are you there!" she screamed at the beauty she couldn't see. Give me some peace, she prayed silently. Let me see something to give me peace or just to let me rest my mind. If the way is through gentleness, show me how to be gentle and not take myself down. If it's strength I need, show me strength that won't make me kill him. Or her.

Orion hadn't known she would meet Brigid again in Santa Cruz, and she had not allowed herself to suspect, when they were at Pacific Pines, how strong the attraction was between them. When she had first fully embraced her, she felt Brigid's body yield to hers, their bodies fluid, accommodating. When she went back to Noe Valley that Sunday, back to Frank, and moved into his arms, into his greeting, it was like a boulder pressing against her, flattening her breasts though he had none. There was no yielding whatsoever.

Yet he never broke. When Orion got arrested, he had worried, but then he picked her up from the city jail, dropped her off at home and went to play golf. He pared the course that day, too. The day he found out about Brigid, he had come close to breaking, to letting his heart be broken, but he had pulled in his reserves once more, and that night he won a hundred dollars at poker, the most he'd ever won, more than any of his buddies had won in one night in all the years they'd been playing together. How did he do it? He'd say he made lemonade out of lemons. What do I make? Chaos out of order. Bombed out bridges.

She had walked ten miles that day, and ten miles the day before. She wasn't tired. Anger had her racing along the trail. Sometimes even uphill she'd find herself running. A few times she'd stumbled and banged herself up. She didn't care about that at all, except that those encounters with the world outside did seem to lessen, for a few moments anyway, the searing pains and silent howls in her sinews.

She remembered this. She remembered doing just this a long time ago in the alley by Mrs. Martin's house. Oh, Orion thought, I am still Carol, crazy as ever, maybe even crazier. I have not changed. Thousands of dollars and thousands of hours spent on therapy, and the only progress I've made is that now I don't have to get drunk to get crazy.

CHAPTER THREE

Who That Girl Had Been

Hey. You sure got stoned fast. Here." Denise returned the cigarette to Carol, who took a half-hearted drag and sat back on her bed. She was thinking about how nice the clerk at the drugstore had been and how mean she was for stealing the inhalers from his store. Well, his dad could probably afford it. What the hell. And there was something about stealing that she found thrilling, though the feeling didn't seem to last very long. It was the same with smoking joints. She'd only been doing it for a year, but already she could feel the intensity lessening, sometimes she was nearly bored with it. "Not thrilling," she said aloud, forgetting, not for the first time, that Denise was there.

She looked at her curtains. Stealing the material had been a little too thrilling. The night watchman didn't really pass out the way he was supposed to. Lillie said that when she had worked days they would find him, almost every morning, lying on top of one of the stacks. The factory cat, which was supposed to be keeping the mice away, was often passed out on the guard's belly. The girls figured he was sharing his booze with the cat. It made some of the girls mad. Lillie thought it was cute.

When Lillie started working nights, she'd kept her eye on the man, and she'd noted when it was that he came around, about what time he'd start weaving a little, and then what time he would disappear—usually around eleven—not to be seen again till morning. "All you needed to know," she said, "was where he was sleeping it off."

The plan Carol devised with Lillie was for Lillie to stay at the shop after she clocked out and to hide in the Ladies Room where there was a pay phone and where he probably wouldn't go, if he hadn't already passed out anyway. Nobody would be back till eight in the morning, so they would have plenty of time, and Carol wanted plenty of time to pick out exactly the material she wanted and in the right amounts. No hurry.

At midnight, if everything was okay, Lillie was to call the Home, ring twice, hang up, wait ten minutes, then call again and hang up. The plan was precise and, Carol thought, foolproof.

Now as Carol looked at the curtains she admitted that she hadn't needed the curtains, really, but she was glad that she had found a way to get them, to get something that she really wanted. She'd done a good job sewing them together by hand. Sometimes, though, like tonight, she didn't feel pride when she looked at them.

Early in the evening before the burglary, Carol had gone

down to the drugstore. She was thinking she'd steal some cough medicine with alcohol or codeine in it, but when she got to the section for cold remedies she saw they had some Benzene Inhalers. The counter boy was stacking candy bars, but he was watching her, too, so Carol went right over to him and quickly checked out which candy wasn't in the stack he was putting up.

"Can I help you?" he asked.

"Yeah," she said. "Don't you have any Snickers?"

The boy sighed. "Yeah, they're still in the back. I was going to get them on my next trip." He was a cute guy, blonde, the owner's son, Carol figured. She smiled at him and he smiled back. "But it's no trouble. I'll go bring some out. Be back in a minute."

Carol waited till she was sure he was all the way in the back. Then, trying not to look too deliberate, in case anyone else might be watching her, she walked back to the cold remedies and fixed the position of the inhalers on the second shelf. Then she pretended to look for something on the top shelf while she slipped three inhalers into her pocket and rearranged the rest. She stepped back as the boy approached her, and she noted that nothing looked missing.

"Looking for something there?" the boy was next to her.

"Gee, don't you guys have nothing out here I want? I'm looking for some cough medicine that doesn't have any alcohol or codeine in it."

The boy shook his head and sighed again. "The stuff for infants? It's in the back, too."

"Oh, never mind. I'll get it next time."

The boy smiled again. He looked at her as if she were a really nice girl not to make him go back there and find it. "It's no trouble."

Carol took the Snickers bar and gave the boy some money. "Next time. I'm in a hurry tonight, but thanks."

She left the store feeling angry. She'd done what she wanted to do, but the boy was so nice. She hated these soft feelings in herself.

"What're you doing?" Denise roused herself.

"Making a cocktail."

You keeping it all to yourself?"

"Well, I thought you were asleep."

Denise sat up straight and watched Carol draw the cotton out of the plastic container and then squeeze it so that the Benzedrine dripped out of the cotton into a glass of warm water. Carol didn't know what else they put into the inhaler, but it smelled a lot like Pine Sol. She inhaled deeply first, just the vapors. Then she sipped the water ceremoniously, sloshed it around on her tongue and over her teeth, and swallowed.

Denise did what Carol did only in such an exaggerated way that it made Carol laugh. "Denise, you look like you're going to spit it out!" That made Denise laugh and she swallowed the wrong way and started coughing wildly. Carol slapped her on the back, and the two girls laughed like any two young girls might laugh who were not planning a burglary.

"Doesn't this make us sort of sisters, or something?"

Carol looked at her.

"I mean drinking from the same glass and doing something daring."

"No. It only seals a pact of silence. A secret. Besides, we haven't done anything daring yet." Carol took another sip of the Benzene water and passed it to Denise. "Here's to our secret. You can never tell anyone. Do you swear?"

"I swear."

Out of a sudden kindness, a desire to make things more equal, Carol said, "I swear, too."

"Well, I didn't know you had to." Then Denise started to say something, but stopped herself.

"What?"

"I just wonder. Why can't you be nice like this all the time?"

Carol started to get angry, but she held herself back, wanting to test the kinder feelings she'd felt just a moment before. "I don't know, Denise. Honestly I don't know." Quickly she stood up. "Let's do something. I'm getting the heebee jeebees just sitting here."

"What do you want to do?"

"I don't know." Carol went over to the window and sat on the casement. She looked out past the dark palms into the night sky. She could see a few stars, not many. A sudden heaviness fell upon her. "Do you have a cigarette?"

Denise got up and handed Carol a cigarette. Carol pulled out her Zippo. She flipped back the top with her thumb and a flick of her wrist. Then she struck the wheel with her thumb, watching the sparks fly and the wick catch. She liked the fumes. She lit her cigarette and inhaled deeply. "If we weren't doing this tonight, I'd sure like to smoke a joint."

"Yeah, well you told me and Lillie you'd kill us if we did."

"Don't worry. I'm not going to." Carol went to her desk and pulled out a pack of cards. "How about Crazy Eights?"

"Okay."

At midnight, exactly, the phone rang. And it rang twice. Same thing at ten after. The girls were out the window and down at the shop in another fifteen. Lillie was at the door waiting for them. She motioned them inside.

"I can't see," Denise whined.

Carol couldn't see either, so she took Lillie's hand in one of hers and Denise's in the other. "Stay calm. Lillie's going to lead us." She squeezed Lillie's hand. "Just hold my hand, Denise, and don't talk."

"My heart's beating so hard," Denise whispered. "Can you hear it?"

"No. Be quiet."

Gradually they worked their way into an area that had a bit of light and followed Lillie through a door. When they shut the door behind them, they were, again, in darkness.

"Lillie, there aren't any windows in here, are there?"

"I don't remember. I don't think so."

"Well, we'll have to take a chance and turn the light on. We can't see what we're doing like this."

"Okay." She felt Lillie move away in search of the light, and she became aware of the trembling in her hand; she didn't know if it was coming from her or from Denise.

Lillie found the light. They were in the storage room where the large remnants and bits and pieces of material were kept that might be put together later for decoration or trim. Most of the fabric was piled neatly; the rest was stacked carelessly here and there, and then there was some that seemed to have been just thrown down onto the floor as if no one knew what to do with it.

"The guard's sleeping it off out in front," Lillie said, "but we have to be quiet. He hasn't locked up much yet and if he wakes up he might come around. He's got a gun, you know."

"Oh, come on. He's not going to shoot three unarmed

teenage girls!" Carol said, but her heart raced and she felt a smile form on her lips as she imagined her picture in the paper, lying dead among the blood-splattered stacks of cloth. She saw through other eyes and felt something triumphant as she felt those eyes leave her picture and go on to another not knowing that the dead girl had been that girl at the Home, or that girl that was here for awhile, or that girl that I gave away.

"Carol. What're you doing?" Lillie hadn't seen Carol's little reveries before.

"Nothing. Let's get started."

"Help yourself."

Carol saw that Denise had already found something she liked, a gold material with a raised design woven into it. "Not that Denise. It's too expensive looking. People will ask you about it. Get something plainer."

"But I like it," Denise protested, and she gathered it tightly to her chest. Carol shot a hard look at Denise and then went on her own search. Almost immediately she saw what she wanted. Broad strips of black cotton stacked neatly next to strips of white cotton. Carol had made measurements of her windows weeks ago when the girls first hatched their plan, and she was about to measure the strips so that she'd be able to calculate how many she'd need of each color, when she saw that Denise was stuck with the gold cloth and wasn't making a move.

"Denise, choose something else. Hurry up." That seemed to be what Denise had been waiting for, just that little bit of attention. Satisfied, she turned and began looking again.

Carol took out her tape measure and made her calculations. Then she quickly counted out the exact number plus a few extra in case she made any mistakes sewing them together. As soon as she had finished counting and stacking her strips, she went over to help Denise.

"How about this pink stuff? It'll go good with the green on your walls."

"It's too sissy."

Just then they heard something. Keys. Without a word, Lillie snapped off the light, and the three girls moved quickly behind the stacks.

The sound of keys was accompanied by uncertain footfalls. It was the guard for sure. They heard a key enter the storeroom door, and they heard the lock turn. Then it turned back again. A sudden push, and a shaft of light entered the room like a dragon. The girls were huddled together, the three of them trembling and passing the motion back and forth from body to body.

"Who's in there?" asked the guard in a surprisingly soft voice. "Kitty? Are you in there, kitty?" From nowhere came the ringing reply of a cat. It had been in the room with the girls the whole time. Carol had to put her hand over her mouth to stop from laughing.

"Come on, kitty. I've got something for you." Carol could see the cat from where she was. It was a skinny gray cat with a drooping belly, and it moved slowly, without eagerness, like Denise. Suddenly the cat stopped and turned, heading straight for the girls.

"Where're you going kitty?" The footsteps and even the whiskey smell of the guard moved closer, within a few feet of them. He leaned down and reached for the cat. The girls sat crouched, ready to spring. Denise let out a tiny gasp. "What? What did you say, kitty?" The cat stopped, turned back to the guard and then, apparently, passed him and went out the door because the guard turned around a bit too quickly and fell upon the stacked material that the girls were hiding behind. He recovered himself quickly, getting his balance and singing out to the kitty again: "Don't run away, kitty. I got a little something for you here, and I know you like it."

The girls heard the guard walk unsteadily toward the door, still talking to the cat. They heard him close the door. Then they heard him lock it.

"Oh, no," Lillie cried in a whisper. "Oh, my god, we're locked in here. I'm going to lose my job. They're going to find us here."

"Wait a minute."

"What?"

"Just be quiet for a second."

The three girls sat there in silence, their legs shaking, their hearts pounding. Slow dark seconds passed. Finally, Carol said, "Okay. I just wanted to be sure he didn't come back for them right away."

"For what?" Denise asked.

"The keys. I think he left the keys in the door."

Carol moved to the door in the darkness. She bent over and looked into the keyhole. Then she snapped on the lights and looked again. "I'm pretty sure they're in there."

Denise and Lillie joined Carol at the door.

"Here's the plan. I'm going to work on getting us out of here and you're going to get the same material I had. Here're the measurements. I already worked it all out. You just get the same number as I did."

"But how'll we get out?"

"Just go do it."

Denise liked the idea—she'd have a room like Carol's. "No," Lillie said, "it'll be too much of the same stuff missing. They'll notice it."

"That's right!" Carol said, hitting her forehead with the ball of her hand. "Christ, I'm stupid." She thought for a moment. "Okay. Lillie will help you find something, Denise. I'll work on the door."

Carol went over to a cardboard box, ripped off a section, slipped it under the door, and then she took her tape measure, flattened out the bent tip with the heel of her shoe, and slipped it into the keyhole.

"Denise was again at her side. "How'd you learn to do that?"

"I thought you were looking for material."

"I'm going. Just want to know."

"Mrs. Martin taught me. Now go."

"That mean old lady you used to live with?"

"Yeah," Carol answered, pushing the girl away. "Now go. I need to concentrate."

The cardboard muffled the sound of the keys when they finally fell out of the lock and onto the floor. Carol wanted to move fast, fast as lightning, but pulled the cardboard back in slowly, careful not to let the keys slip off. The tension was so strong in her body that it almost felt like there was some other hand pulling against hers. Then she had them. She jumped up, whispered to the girls to hide and keep their mouths shut, and flicked the lights off. After a long silence, Carol said, "I think it's okay. He didn't hear anything," and she found her way back to the lights and switched them on. "Look, Lillie, I've got the keys," she said, dangling them in front of the two terrified girls.

"Come on. We've got to get out of here before he notices his keys are missing."

Carol's hands were shaking as she tried the keys in the lock. It seemed like she'd been through them all when finally she felt the snug fit of the right one. The lock turned and snapped open. Lillie and Denise each took some of Carol's material in their arms and, very quietly, very slowly, made their way back along the path that they'd taken coming in.

They had reached the outside door before Carol realized she still had the keys in her hand.

"Shit! I've got to go back."

"Why? He'll never remember where he left them. Let's go. Just put them in the lock here."

"He might remember. He might..." Something stopped Carol. She raised her hand to her mouth and glared at the girls to be quiet. From down the hall they heard the mutterings of the guard. They could hear, "Kitty, where's those keys. Now I know you hid them from me. Did you leave them in the store room, kitty? I'll just bet you did."

They heard the guard turn and go down the hall to the storeroom. "Okay," Carol said softly, "you two go ahead," and they did, the two girls running, the stolen goods held tightly to their breasts.

Carol watched them until they disappeared and everything was quiet again. Then she very slowly opened the door again, and stepped inside. She chose a key, put it in the lock, and though it didn't fit, it did keep the keys suspended from the keyhole. Carefully she slipped through the door again and closed it behind her.

She wanted to walk slowly, to savor all that had happened

and all that she had escaped, but she felt her legs gain speed, and soon she was running. She ran and she laughed and, a few times, she howled, but before she got back to the Home, she felt the good feeling leaving her, and something sad began to worm its way into her heart. She was coming down from the Benzene, too. She felt her teeth chatter. She needed something to help her down. She should have stolen some of that cough medicine.

CHAPTER FOUR

Giving Up Comfort

Orion camped near Summit Lake. After she had put the tent up, she went to gather kindling and dry branches for a fire. It was what she'd always done with Frank. Put up the tent, then go, he in one direction, she in another, to find wood. How she wished, now, that when she got back he would be there. "Idiot," she said aloud. She could remember, if she would only try to be a little more realistic, how awful it was to walk always in silence and even to sit in silence by the fire. He didn't seem ever to want her to be there with him. She smiled, realizing that must be what it had felt like to be Denise.

She remembered once, as she and Frank were watching the fire together, she felt a longing to be invisible, not just to seem that way, but to be absolutely gone—to be released like the smoke that was wafting up through the trees into the atmosphere, into the cool dark sky. The stars were brilliant in the night sky, and suddenly her longing became so intense she felt she might actually disappear, and it scared her. She looked over at Frank, thinking she'd find a way to not be alone with this feeling. She was surprised to see that he was engaged in a very lively way with something going on in the fire. Something happening, she thought, that he might not mind telling her about. She risked crossing the silence.

"The stars are beautiful tonight."

He glanced up and then quickly returned his gaze to the fire. "I was just looking at the wood burning. I see a rabbit with its ears sticking up. It's being swallowed by a wolf or something."

"Where?" she nearly shouted.

"Oh, it's just below the big log. You can't really see it now."

She knew better than to insist, and quickly he returned to his silence, maybe went deeper into it. He was not peaceful. He was inert.

"Waiting like a dog," she said to the bundle of wood in her arms. How could she wait around like that, hoping he'd let her in.

Three or four times every summer for as long as they were married they had backpacked somewhere in California, and even though they didn't talk, she felt she learned something new about him and about herself, almost always something good: patience, intelligence, strength. She rarely showed her fears. He seemed not to have any. She wondered, at times, if she had seemed too tough for him, not feminine, but she felt, instinctively, that it was better to err on the side of strength.

Orion's long hikes in the Marble Mountains that day and the day before made her feel good. It was right that her body was struggling the way her spirit had been struggling all these weeks. Now she was going down to the lake to catch a fish. She had always left that to him.

She dropped the wood off by the tent, picked up her gear, and went down to the lake. She pulled out the container that held the worms and tried not to wince as she separated one worm from the tangle of worms and put it onto the hook. She made a fair cast and let the line float out, half hoping nothing would bite. Almost immediately she felt a tug on her line. She was going to catch a fish. She reeled in slowly, as he would probably have done, keeping the line taut, making steady progress. Then, suddenly, the line went dead, and she thought she'd lost her fish.

She hadn't. In a second, it leaped into the air and then back into the water and started to fight, splashing water then going quiet and then splashing some more. She let it play out a little and then held her line and slowly, very carefully and slowly, she pulled it in. When she raised it out of the water, it started fighting again, and she didn't have a net to catch it, so she grabbed it and for one brief moment it was still, one eye directly on her. Then it leaped out of her hand and fought the air, landing on the ground. She grabbed the line, jerked the fish back up into the air and then let it thrash and flail as she walked away from the lake toward a rock.

She had seen him do it. She could do it. She grabbed the fish again, and this time she held onto it. With her knife she cut the line. Then she raised the fish up by its tail, hesitated for just a second, and then, with all her might, whacked its head against the rock. It dangled there from her hand, dead.

She cleaned the fish, cutting it open, gutting it. She could feel her stomach start to heave, so she sang to take her mind off what she was doing: "Flip a switch, turn a dial, that's modern living, electric style." A dragonfly hovered near. It moved like a helicopter, and it was the right colors, aqua blue and black. It would stop in mid-air, then jerk forward and stop again. It seemed to be looking at itself in the soft metallic surface

of the lake. Orion had an infant's urge to grab and crush it, and even moved her hand toward it, but it went into gear and out of reach.

She took her shoes off and dangled her feet in the water. She'd broken into a sweat and the snowmelt lake calmed her as it cooled her. The sun was setting. Small winged insects flew out into the slanting light and lit up like dancing stars, millions of them, fluttering out of the scrub brush and pines. The lake was shimmering, too; it caught the sun in a thousand sparkling fists and skimmed it along the surface.

Orion drew her feet, now nearly numb from the cold, out of the water and let them dry in the setting sun as she listened and watched. The sounds gradually changed from the low-pitched flops of the fish leaping about on the lake to the sitar and zither sounds of flying insects. Something flew by—it must have been the quickness of its beating wings—that sounded like her fishing rod clicking back when she drew the line in. Crickets began their metallic twilight song, joined by the croaks and ribits of frogs. Then Orion heard something that seemed to go off like a popgun. She laughed, grabbed her socks and shoes and quickly put them on, and leaped up, a sudden inspiration upon her. She dropped the fish into her daypack and looked around.

She spotted a pine with a broad trunk, drew her knife out and began to carve, knowing it was wrong, destructive. But now, she laughed to herself, I have started a blood thirst. It will be satisfied.

It was almost dark before she finished. She heard the faint rumbling of thunder, as well as the whirps and whipples of the night animals. She stepped back and read the inspiration, which went nearly twice around the tree: "Ravi Shankar loves Spike Jones."

It started to rain, softly, as night came on. The moon had not yet risen. It was dark and suddenly cold. Orion didn't have her parka or her flashlight with her, but even as she stumbled and even as she lost the trail, retraced her steps, found the trail and stumbled some more, there was within her a smile, an approval of her handy work that came from an odd place, an old place.

By the time Orion got back to camp, it was raining hard and it was windy, too. There was nothing she could do in the dark with the rain coming down like that, so she went into the tent, dried herself off a little and found her flashlight. As she directed the light from corner to corner to see if the tent was taking the wind all right, she noticed the rain fly. It was in the tent with her and not over the top of the tent as it should be. At that very instant she felt a single heavy tap on her head. The rain was coming through.

Orion went out into the rain with the fly. She struggled to get it spread out across the top of the tent. The rain was in her eyes, and the wet strings of the fly wouldn't take the knots she tried to make to the tent poles. She had to fight back tears, as well, and it made her angry that she was crying over this little thing. The anger stopped the tears. Finally, she had the rain fly tied into the place. It wasn't on right, but it would be some protection.

Orion crawled back into the tent, sopping wet and full of self hatred. Twenty miles of earth under her feet in two days, catching a fish, hearing the music of the forest, violating the forest, nothing, in the end, had worked to comfort her. It didn't feel like a broken heart, it felt like a heart spiked through. A hook, like the one she'd used on the fish, pierced her heart and made her want to scream out in pain, to push from the inside this thing away from her.

He wanted a divorce, and for some reason that she could not really understand, his wanting a divorce had torn from her any desire to live. Anger seemed to be all that she could call upon to stop her from killing herself. But anger was hard to control and it would take forms: knives, guns, swords, explosives, stabbing, piercing, severing, obliterating him and her who had taken her desire to live. And they'd done it so calmly, so reasonably. She had been bad. She had been needy. She had not been reasonable.

What did I expect him to do? I think I thought he would find a way to see me through it. I didn't think he'd just look out for himself. Wasn't I worth some effort from someone who said he loved me? How could he just cut his losses and run. This man who could play any game, physical or mental, for hour upon hour upon tournament hour. Why hadn't he had the strength to see her through? Was he just lazy about love? Was it too much trouble?

By now Orion could feel her teeth chatter, she was shaking from the cold and from anger.

I'll die in this tent. Could I die in this tent? I could stab myself with my Swiss Army knife. I could just take all my clothes off and lie outside in the rain and die of exposure."

Orion wondered if she could die of fear, of the fear she'd kept with her all the years since she'd escaped from the Home.

The fear that had kept her tight and tidy and pleasant. Her good grades in high school and college, her scrubbed and polished home, her perfect dinners for her perfect husband and his friends—they had all kept the fear down, kept the nuns and the police and everyone and everything that had ever wanted to harm her—kept it all at bay. "I want a divorce," he said, and all that hard work lifted and flew away like a bird from a magician's hat, and in the hat, another creature stirred. Then it rose and coiled around her heart, pierced it, filled it with venom and then entered. That was it. A snake at the center of her life, eating its way out from the inside.

She smiled. "When they find me here dead, Frank will say, 'I'll bet she didn't put the rain fly on.' And his girlfriend will say, in her new-age therapy talk, as they rebirth themselves in a Jacuzzi, 'It must have been what she really wanted. Some day, Frank, you'll see it was cosmically perfect.' And of course, someday, maybe even that very day, he would. And, Orion noted, they would never admit to themselves that they were happy she was dead. That would be a bad thought.

How often, it seemed to her, the reasonable, even the honorable thing, nay, the only thing civilized people like them could do under the circumstances, was also the most self-serving, the easiest thing to do.

Frank knew the rules and played by them, belonged to that group of reasonable men who made the rules with the sure unspoken instinct that made them always come out on top. So clear in reason, he had no room for struggle. He did not know what his feelings were, and readily admitted it; in fact, he seemed proud of it.

Frank had liked it when they first met that she was able to

interpret behavior, anticipate needs, note what pleased or displeased, could tell when something was wrong. It confused Carol, as she had not had much experience with men like Frank, that he thought she was very skillful in these ways. She thought these were normal natural abilities, and she half doubted that he didn't actually have them himself. She thought maybe he simply chose not to bother, but then again, maybe it was possible that somehow he had never been pushed into learning these things, that he had been very lucky in life. But a few times she thought, no, he is not lucky, he is even lonelier than I am. That thought had made his ignorance and silence more bearable.

But today she could kill him for not knowing his own feelings. He was irresponsible in this. It made him fearful. It made him unable to help her. He stood for a few months at a distance watching her go off to the therapist, expecting her to somehow come home cured and ready to resume their life together or to end it. Waiting, a reasonable length of time, for her to get things straight in her head. But she knew, at bottom, it was all too much for him. It had to do with things he knew nothing about and didn't want to know. He stood at this distance and watched for as long as a decent man would; then turned and fell into the arms of the cheerleader. No one could blame him.

"I should kill them both." She could see them lying there very clearly, their designer clothes covered with blood, his frown, her smile, at last and forever altered by something real.

The innocents, knowing only what they have to know to appear human, protecting themselves from knowing, killing the rest of us by their negligence, wondering why we can't be strong like them. And we, the further we are flung from the center, wondering the same thing, wondering if they aren't possibly right to not see, not hear, not speak, and to feel nothing except occasional pity and the constant strong pull toward the center. This center is not filled with fire. It is ice, sheer and sharp, and also bedrock. The axis of the earth cannot loose itself from the center, and we turn and turn upon this powerful frozen core of willful ignorance.

And then, she thought, it wouldn't be fitting to leave them out there in the open, naked, as they had never been in life.

But I do not want to exalt them. I'll cover Frank with his high school letterman jacket and whatshername with pompoms.

"Please," she prayed aloud, "whatever's out there, let me not kill them. Let me live through this without killing them."

Orion didn't have any cigarettes with her. No drugs. No booze. No therapist. Nothing. And when she let her anger weaken, then there would be no cushion between her and the shame she felt that she had lost everything and everyone over and over and over.

With nothing to drink or smoke, she was as alone with this terrible nature of hers. She felt she could die from shame.

When morning came, she found that she hadn't died. She had suspected she wouldn't when, sometimes during the night, she had awakened, and there was no sound of rain, and she had changed into dry clothes, and then found her sleeping bag, and it was dry. She climbed into it for warmth, not thinking that she'd sleep again, but she did.

She had made it through the night, but she felt no gratitude. She went outside and saw that there was a puddle of rain on the fly and that the fly looked like it had been put on by someone completely deranged. Well.

Orion remembered the fish. She got it out of her pack, went

down to the lake with it, and threw it back in, hoping that even headless and gutless, it would be food for something in there. She felt no hunger herself, no thirst. She washed her hands and face. Then she went back to the campsite, got her notebook out and wrote: "I grieve the love I've lost, but much more I grieve the love I never had, the love I hoped was mine, the humiliation of being found out, the mistake I made thinking it was mine, that it was meant for me. I was needy, foolish. I grieve the love I do not have in me. I have anger. It has filled the empty place. It has been my abiding comfort. Now, if I have any hope of redemption, I will have to give that up, too."

CHAPTER FIVE

A Jump in the Lake

Carol's eyes fell back to the dried stems and leaves in the lid of the shoe box. She picked the stems out and lightly crushed the leaves between her fingers. Then she took a match book cover, opened it and began pushing the rough leaves up toward the top end of the lid, allowing the seeds to roll down, away from the tobacco.

The leaves were not brown. They weren't green, either, but some color like the old Army blankets that covered most of the beds in the Home. Or, she thought, as she felt the slightly sticky residue left on her fingers, the color of the dark Italian oil Mario put on his bread.

It was good Mario was there, Carol thought, as she took two rolling papers, opened them, and piggy-backed one on top of the other so that two gummed edges showed. She filled the paper with the tobacco and rolled it into a cigarette between her fingers. Then she licked the edges of the paper and patted them into place. She was pleased with the snug fit of the tobacco in the paper, with the uniformity of the cigarette, top to bottom. She had only to cap the ends.

"What are you smiling about?" Denise broke into Carol's thoughts.

"A good job. I just did a good job." Carol held the thin brown cigarette up for Denise to admire. "Should I cap it or are you ready for more?"

"We still got this one, Carol." Denise handed what was left of the first cigarette back to Carol.

Carol took a toke and passed the tiny roach back to Denise. "I don't need anymore," she said, crimping the ends of the newly rolled cigarette with one of her drawing pencils.

"I wish you wouldn't do that. I can't get them open right."

"Well, you just use your thumb, see?" Carol demonstrated.

"Yeah, I seen you do that before, but it never comes out right for me; just fold it over. Okay?"

"Okay."

"You're in a pretty good mood, huh?"

"Why?"

"Well, I got some bad news. I mean sort of bad."

Carol waited.

"Well, do you want to know what it is?"

"Yeah."

"Okay. I'll tell you. At dinner Sister Mary Joan made an announcement. She said that they're repairing the roofs at Immaculata and for about two weeks the girls are going to come and live here. They're going to stay with us."

"What do you mean? Stay in the Home? Where?"

"That's what I'm trying to tell you. They're going to stay in our rooms, right in our rooms with us."

Carol said nothing, but she looked at Denise, afraid to ask if she was going to have to be her roommate. Denise was a pretty sorrowful case. Her hair was never washed. It hung, in oily dark blonde strands, around her eyes and lapped around her neck. Her neck and face were pink, blotchy, and her eyes were a pale sad brown. She squinted a lot. She needed glasses but wouldn't wear the ones she could get through the Home.

Denise was pointy. Her elbows and knees and nose, her cheekbones, were thinly covered with flesh; it seemed to have been stretched over her.

"Are you going to be my roommate?"

"That's the worst part. We have to be roommates with the convent girls!"

"No!"

"Yes. Sister Mary Joan said so. I knew you wouldn't like no stranger in your room, and I told Sister Mary Joan we'd rather be roommates, but she said they all got together and thought it would be good for us and them to mix so that we could know each other and understand… something, I don't know."

"When are they coming?"

"Next Friday."

"Oh, no," Carol said, closing her eyes, picturing the clean cut big-toothed, pasty little snob she'd have for a roommate. Carol, of course, had seen the girls of Immaculata at basketball games and other competitions and at the mixers all the Catholic schools in the area forced their students to attend once or twice a year.

Carol smiled and shook her head thinking of how the Immaculata girls and Cathedral boys danced—with their rumps sticking out. If they touched, would that be a sin of the flesh or a sin of what they thought when they touched? Did they commit sins of thought? Did they let their bodies talk to their brain? It seemed to Carol that when they embraced out there on the dance floor they became less aware of each other and more aware of themselves, of their feet and knees, elbows and shoulders, as if that was where they danced from and as if they were not a boy and a girl in each other's arms.

Whatever it was they were doing out there, it had its effect on Carol and the other girls and boys who were not from Immaculata or Cathedral. When they slow-danced they were like interlocking pieces of a jigsaw puzzle. But at the mixers they themselves became self-conscious, started dancing apart and from their feet and elbows. It was no fun at all. You couldn't lose yourself for a minute.

Carol saw the cultured pearls and cashmere sweaters. She saw the clearness of their skin and eyes, the straight long shimmering hair, the white teeth that seemed always to be showing. She thought she was prepared for what was coming, but the girl she opened her door to was unlike anyone she had ever seen.

She had curly hair. It was dark red. Her eyes were brown with an amber light in them. Her skin, fair, but not pale. In fact, to Carol it was a warm color, like honey.

The girl was beautiful, but what really stunned Carol was the way she moved into the room, the way she took up space. She knew she belonged to the world, that she had a right to things.

Carol glanced at the name tag on the girl's luggage, but she'd never seen that name before and wasn't sure how to pronounce it. "You take the bed," was all she could think to say.

The girl started to protest. Carol interrupted: "Sister said. All the visitors are supposed to have the beds. We get the cots. We're supposed to be 'gracious.'"

The girl laughed out loud. "You've got a good sense of humor," she said, and Carol looked at her to read the attitude behind the words. There was no mockery or ridicule that she could detect. "They told us," the girl went on, "that we're not supposed to be patronizing or condescending and that we shouldn't wear expensive clothes."

Carol noted the words that the girl used and would look them up later, but she could see from the girl's manner that she was being spoken to nicely. She looked at the pearls and the sweater.

"I know. But I figured these are my clothes. These are the things I wear. If I brought in just old raggedy stuff, that wouldn't be honest. Besides," and here she gave Carol a long sweet look, "I wouldn't be fooling you, would I?"

Carol felt a sudden shyness, but immediately broke through it, extending her hand. "My name's Carol."

"My name's Dierdra," the girl said, taking Carol's hand in hers.

*   *   *   *   *

"The first girl I ever loved had an Irish name. It was Dierdra."

Brigid raised herself up onto one elbow and looked quizzically at Orion. "So, I'm not the first woman in your life, after all?"

"I hadn't thought of her, till now, as a woman in my life. It's funny. We made love all right, but I didn't think of us as lovers. If I thought about it at all, I'd probably just have considered it something happening in my life which, it seemed to me even then, was different from everyone else's. There was a sort of real reality and then there was the one I was living in. It was something like a corridor that ran off to the side somehow." Carol smiled. "I'd heard the word 'queer,' of course. I knew there were queers, but they were men. Women were sort of non-sexual. We just weren't—"

"Conscious." Brigid leaned over and kissed Orion on the forehead. "May you be blessed with consciousness from now on."

"Will it hurt?"

"A lot." Brigid looked at Orion tenderly. "Tell me about Dierdra."

"Okay," Orion said, but she found she couldn't just jump into those memories. She looked away from Brigid and concentrated on the scene framed in the window. Black oak, blue sky, and a very distant pale green stretch of the Pacific Ocean. She gave herself some time to move back, to try again to be close to Dierdra and to stay calm at the same time.

"What's the first thing you remember?"

"How much I wanted her."

Brigid howled and laughed, suddenly a very young girl.

"How old were you?"

"Thirteen, I think. Yeah."

"How old was she?"

"Not much older, fourteen or fifteen."

"And you knew right away?"

"Well, let's say within a week. Maybe less. I mean those were the very words that went through my head: "I want her. I hadn't known that feeling before. Sure, I knew how you make babies, I knew how you could do things. But making love, loving someone with your body, loving them, their body. I didn't know. But with this girl…"

"Were you scared?"

"Probably not. I mean, those days, I was very different. If I had been afraid, I'd have been the last to know it."

*   *   *   *   *

Dierdra held Carol's hand for what seemed a long time. Maybe she imagined it. The girls released their hands and then simultaneously went to pick up Deirdre's suitcase. The back of their hands brushed together, and Carol felt it in her legs.

"Here let me get it," Carol said, swinging the suitcase onto the bed."

"Oh, it'll ruin your beautiful bedspread."

"It doesn't matter. You like it?" Dierdra nodded. "I made it."

"You did?"

"Yeah. I made the curtains, too."

"Gee, they're really, really nice. I can't believe it." Dierdra went over and took the curtains in her hands, examining them. "What fine work. You must have a lot of patience."

Carol laughed. "No one ever said that about me before! I wouldn't be in this place if I had any patience at all."

"But you must have," Dierdra insisted, showing Carol the small stitches so neatly

placed. "Look on the outside and you can hardly tell if it's two pieces sewn together or just one."

"Well, hummm Carol hesitated, unsure of how to take this

praise and shy again and having to break through the shyness. "Maybe I do have some patience sometimes… when it's things. Not when it's people, though." Carol looked away from Dierdra, feeling now more deeply shy, frightened really, by the girl's ability to see and then, without missing a beat, to come right out and say what she saw. Carol wondered: If Dierdra looked straight into my eyes, what would she see?

"You don't know how to take a compliment, do you?"

Carol needed to slow her new roommate down and she shot out with too much energy: "I can take a compliment. I can take anything."

"Whoa! Sorry. I guess I ask too many questions."

"No. I'm just not used to you yet."

"Good. Then I can ask questions?"

"Sure," Carol said, but she was aware of the breath going out of her and she could still feel the girl's hand brushing against hers. The two girls were standing, simply looking at each other, about to speak, when they heard the dinner bell. It was past dinner, but it was the bell calling them to assemble.

There were welcoming speeches by the welcoming officials of Father Junipero Serra—the Mother Superior of the girls' school and the priest who was Director of the boys' school, though there weren't any boys involved in this project. The Monsignor also said a few words. What Carol noticed were not the words—they were the same as always—but the way they spoke when they addressed the girls from Immaculata: They were all smiles and apologies. Carol had never seen them that way before, and she was embarrassed. Didn't they care that the rest of us were watching them while they acted like morons around these girls?

Carol said something to Dierdra about it after dinner. They were back in Carol's room, sitting on either end of the bed. "I never saw Mother Superior smile like that before. She's really happy to have you here I guess."

"Maybe she's just nervous. You know they talked to us a long time about coming here before we finally decided to do it."

"Who decided?"

"All of us. The nuns and the girls and Father John."

"Father John?"

"Do you know Father John?" Carol was confused, but managed to nod. "He's really cute, don't you think?" Carol nodded again. "He teaches Religion and some of the science courses at Immaculata and some of the boys' schools. I think he used to come down here to St. Teresa's didn't he?"

"A long time ago. Yeah, I remember him." Then Carol shifted back. "Anyway, what did they say to you?"

"Just sort of preparing us for the worst."

"Like what?"

Dierdra stopped for a moment, reached over, and touched Carol lightly on the arm. "You're angry about something now, aren't you?"

And Carol surprised herself with her own honesty: "Yeah, I am, but I don't know what it is exactly. Something about how you're treated by everyone," and she could have added, 'even by me,' but she stopped short and changed course. "Well, I wont let it bother me. It'll pass."

"Do they beat you?"

Carol laughed. "No! They wouldn't do that. They tell you how 'impossible' you are. That means they're getting ready to say you're 'incorrigible,' and if they say that, it means they're thinking of making you leave the Home, probably going to send you to juvenile hall. Anyway, it's like a sentence to be 'incorrigible,' and I always get the feeling they want to say that, but instead they say 'impossible'. They let you know—without coming right out and saying it—that it's your own fault you never got adopted."

"Why didn't you?"

"According to them or according to me?"

"You."

"Because I didn't want to be."

"Why not?"

"I was in enough foster homes to know I didn't want to live with anyone who isn't really my mother or father," and again Carol could have added something, but didn't because she was told over and over again it was a silly useless idea.

But here was Dierdra, seeing everything and saying, "You think your parents will come back and get you someday?"

Carol felt like she'd been slapped or trapped or both. How did she know? Carol laughed out loud. "No. How dumb do you think I am? They wouldn't be coming back for me after all these years. I mean if they were going to come back for me they would have done it long ago. They're probably dead by now, anyway."

"Oh, don't say that!"

"Why not?"

"It isn't nice to talk like that."

"Well, didn't they tell you before you came—when you were all having your long discussions and voting and all—didn't they tell you we weren't nice?"

But Dierdra wasn't daunted. "You've got a real chip on your shoulder, haven't you?"

"Yeah. Want to knock it off?"

And then Dierdra did the strangest thing. She sat forward and very quickly kissed Carol's shoulder, and then just as quickly she sat back on her end of the bed. "There. Now it's all gone," and both Carol and Dierdra smiled, but Carol was shocked. And thrilled. She really liked this girl.

Things seem to go smoothly after that, and the girls found that it was easy for them to talk to each other. Carol wondered if it was ever difficult for Dierdra to talk to anyone or be anywhere. She was so beautiful and so smart and so self-assured, but in a nice way.

The girls talked until dawn, and Carol noticed that Dierdra was careful when she talked about her mother and father and the things she had. And Dierdra seemed genuinely interested in the fact that Carol worked at a real job and stayed out late and drank and smoked. Carol didn't tell her about the marijuana that Denise had given her as a sort of payment for cleaning and rolling the stuff her brother had given her. Nor did Carol tell her any of the really unhappy stories of foster homes, not only because she thought Dierdra wouldn't like them—they weren't nice—but also because she was ashamed of those experiences. So Carol told Dierdra the other stories about foster homes, about the brothers and sisters she'd had for months or years. And any funny stories she remembered, she told, but mostly the girls stayed clear of home and family and talked about their futures, what they were going to do with their lives.

"I want to build houses," Carol said.

"Do you want to really build them or just design them?"

"Both. I want to do everything. I want to make all the furniture, too, and just do everything exactly the way I want it."

"I want to be a nurse or maybe even a doctor. I'm not sure if my grades will be good enough to get into medical school, though."

"I'll bet you're smart. Don't you get good grades?"

"Yeah, but I have to work really hard."

"You do?"

"Yeah."

"Do you study a lot?"

"Yeah. Don't you?"

"No. I can't. It makes me crazy. I told you I don't have much patience."

"Then how are you going to be a carpenter and an architect and an interior decorator and everything?"

Carol had never put names to her thoughts about what she wanted to do. It sounded frightening. "Well, maybe I won't study those things. Maybe I'll just do them."

Dierdra smiled. "It wouldn't surprise me. There are people who just do things without studying them much. I'm not like that. I'm helpless unless I read a book that tells me how to do something. That's why I can't sew."

"Anybody can sew."

"You make clothes, too?"

"Sure."

"I'll bet you don't even follow a pattern, do you?"

"To tell you the truth, I can't. I don't understand the directions. I mean they have a certain way of talking… it's like they're not talking to you. You know, it's like a teacher saying things but not really saying them to you. I can never understand what people mean when they talk like that."

"So how do you do it?"

"Make clothes? I use newspapers. I cut out the pieces and try them on and then I pin them to the material and cut them out and then I sew it together really loosely. If it fits and when I can find a sewing machine to use, I sew it up. Sew it up twice so it'll be good and strong at the seams."

"Who taught you how to do all that?"

Carol laughed. "No one. Everyone. Just keep my eyes open."

"How did you think to use newspapers?"

"I don't know. It just came to me. Or maybe I saw it somewhere at one of the homes I stayed in. I don't remember, but it's such an easy thing."

"Oh, no it's not. You're really talented."

"You're not trying to make fun of me are you?"

"Goodness no!"

Carol could see Dierdra meant it. "Okay, tell me something you're good at. Something that just comes naturally."

"Ping pong."

"Ping pong! Great. I love to play ping pong. We can play next week down at Echo Park."

"Isn't it dangerous to go down there?"

And here Carol really laughed. "Dangerous? It's a recreation center. Nothing but kids and counselors and some old guys playing dominoes. They have boats down there, too, and we could go out on the lake."

"Can you swim?"

"Sort of. Well, I don't drown anyway. I'll bet you had lessons." Dierdra smiled her admission. God, what a smile.

The next morning, after breakfast, Dierdra's parents came to get her. She would be gone till Sunday night, and Carol would miss her and smoke a lot of dope and talk to herself as she washed dishes down at the Harmony House and then later as she went cruising down to Chavez Ravine and then out to the beach with the gang of girls she knew from Echo Park. And she wondered if she was dangerous.

Sunday night, after dinner, Carol couldn't decide what to do with herself, whether to stay in and wait or go out and not think about Dierdra at all. She went out—down to the park to see if any of the girls were there—but they weren't. The girls usually went to evening mass because they'd sleep too late to make mass in the morning. Even if they had been at the park, Carol wouldn't have been able to not think about Dierdra. She fed the ducks popcorn, and she thought about her. She wondered what it could be that was dangerous about herself or maybe it was just something in the park that Dierdra thought was dangerous.

She watched some younger kids—boys—jumping off the bridge into the lake, shouting, "Cannonball! Let's see you do a cannonball." The boys would jump and then pull their legs up to their chest so that when they hit the water it splashed really high. It looked like fun, and she knew it was against the park rules which made it even more fun. Someone started yelling at them to get out. Then she saw two park policemen walking toward the bridge. One of them ran up onto the bridge and chased the boys off while the other one waited for the kids who were still in the water to swim his way. The kids hadn't realized there were two and they were surprised when they got out of the water to fall into the policeman's grip. Carol couldn't hear what the officer said, but she saw the boys look down at their feet and shake their heads or nod their heads, and then they were let go. They moved away quickly, but they didn't run. Were those kids dangerous?

Carol stopped when she reached the old men playing dominoes. She watched them for a while and then continued on. She saw a lot of families packing up their picnics, leaving for home. She thought about Dierdra's home. She had her own bedroom and a separate room that she could use just to study and then another room just to go watch television and then another room they called the recreation room. That was where they had their own ping pong table. "Wonder if she's really good?" Carol said aloud to the ducks on the edge of the lake. She saw some hoboes here and there looking through the trashcans, and she wondered if this was the danger Dierdra talked about. It didn't seem likely. By now she was back at the bridge. She looked all around and could see no danger. "Maybe it's me, after all," she said. Then she climbed up on the railing and screamed as she cannonballed into the lake.

When Carol got back, Dierdra was there.

"What happened to you?"

"I jumped in the lake at Echo Park." Carol grabbed a towel. "I'm going to take a shower. Are you going to be here?"

"Yeah. Sure. Of course. Why'd you jump in the lake?"

"No reason. Just felt like it. I'll be right back."

As she showered Carol smiled to herself. She's happy to see me. She thinks I'm a little nuts, but she likes me. I can see it in her eyes. Then Carol sang to herself, "They're cooking with Crisco from New York to Frisco."

When she got back, Dierdra was waiting. "I missed you," she said. "Did you miss me over the weekend?"

The question seemed innocent enough but, still, Carol found herself stammering: "I…of course…well I was busy. I worked at the Harmony yesterday and today, and last night I went out with some friends from the park. And then today, well, I went swimming. How was your weekend?"

"Really boring. I couldn't wait to get back."

"Are you kidding?"

"No, really. I missed you."

Again Carol didn't know what to say.

Dierdra stood up and got something out from behind a pillow and put it behind her back. "I brought you something."

"What?"

"Guess what hand."

"The right hand."

Carol thought she saw Dierdra change hands before she drew out the gift and said, "It's a teddy bear. I hope you like it."

Carol took the stuffed animal into her arms and held it, and she felt her throat constrict. She didn't want to make a fool of herself, so she took the bear and put it up on her desk and swallowed and cleared her throat. "There," she said. "It looks good there, don't you think?" She took a deep breath and turned back to Dierdra.

"I didn't get you anything."

"Oh, I didn't expect you to, and it's not new or anything. I just wanted to give you something that meant something to me. I've had that bear since I was a child. I have other ones, too, but that one's… I don't know. I thought you'd like it."

"I do. Really. I was just surprised. Thank you."

And again things were easy between them, and they sat and talked and laughed till it was very late at night. Then they whispered across to each other in the dark. Finally, finally, they slept.

This was a pattern they followed night after night, causing them to be very sleepy in the morning and very sleepy in class all day, but they could not stop. No matter how tired they were, when they saw each other again in the evening they were unable to say enough or hear enough or laugh enough to satisfy themselves.

*   *   *   *   *

When they made love, Brigid screamed. She screamed whatever it was she wanted to scream, sometimes words, sometimes just screaming screams. Orion thought that those screams had to be heard all over the mountains and down to the sea, and they pierced her heart, broke it open, summoned groans of passion from her own throat and made her wild with the knowledge that she had brought this ecstasy to another human being. She wanted to do it again, now.

"Can I make love to you first, before I finish this story?"

"While you finish this story. Tell me what you wanted from her and let me give it to you."

Orion stood up and left their bed, went across the room and sat down, keeping eye contact and not smiling. "First thing I wanted was to see her naked. I wanted to be able to see her without having to smile or notice if she was smiling. I wanted to be able to look at her body the way I wanted to look at her body—I wanted to concentrate on it and not be distracted by her looking at me to see how I was looking at her or having to look at her in a way that would tell her I liked what I saw. I just wanted to look at her and be however I felt like being."

"Tell me what to do."

"Face the wall. Yes. Now, throw back the covers. Good. Now put your right arm along your side."

"Like this?"

"Yes." Orion looked at Brigid for a long time in silence. Then she said, "Turn around and face me, but keep your eyes closed." Orion followed the flowing lines, the sensuous curves, that led from Brigid's forehead to her nose to her lips and chin, and she circled her own breast and wet her lips with her tongue as she looked at Brigid's breasts and saw the nipples were taut. She wanted to lick them. Then she wanted to bite into the sweet valley between her ribs and her hip. "Oh, God, you're beautiful." She followed the ascent and descent of Brigid's hip down to her feet.

"Spread your legs. I want to see."

Dierdra spread her legs. "I want to watch you looking."

"Okay. I won't look at your eyes."

"Good."

"Now take your hand and touch yourself."

Brigid touched herself.

"Do you want my tongue in there?"

Brigid gasped. "You know I do."

Now Orion looked into Brigid's eyes and began to move toward her as she let out a yell: "Eeeyeow" she screamed as she pounced onto Brigid who howled with laughter and then suddenly turned and pinned Orion onto her back. Then less quickly she moved up onto Orion's breast and then further, holding herself just above Orion's mouth. "Is this what you want?"

*   *   *   *   *

Carol sat in the chair a long time. She'd gotten back late, but she still wasn't sleepy. She was, suddenly, dying of hunger. Dierdra had left the desk lamp on, and there was just enough light for Carol to hunt around in her dresser and find some potato chips. She tried to eat them quietly just in case Dierdra was really asleep. She looked over at Dierdra for the hundredth time. She was wearing a baby doll nightgown and she was facing the wall. The gown was up over her hips; the panties matched the gown, and they had little ribbons on them. Carol wanted to touch them. She rose and stepped over to Dierdra. Then quickly she covered Dierdra with the blanket. Immediately, Dierdra turned toward Carol and began talking, a false sleepiness in her voice.

"Hi. What time is it? Is it time to get up?"

"No. I'm just getting in. Go back to sleep."

"What time is it?"

"Late. Were you really asleep?"

"Where'd you go?"

"The usual. Chavez Ravine. Cruising. You know."

"I'd like to go with you sometime."

"I don't think you'd get along with my friends."

"I get along with Denise."

"She's not really my friend. She's just someone I let come along."

"Am I your friend?"

The two girls looked at each other in silence. Finally Carol answered, "Of course you are. What a question!"

"Well, you've been acting kind of like you're angry at me or something. You hardly ever spend time here anymore."

"Neither do you. You're always at school."

Silence again.

"There's something wrong, isn't there, between us, I mean."

"I don't think so. Anyway, we've just got another week. I

think we'll live."

"You know I've already been here two weeks."

"Yeah, I know."

"I should be leaving now."

"I know. Guess it's taking them a lot longer than they thought to fix the roof."

"Are you glad I'm still here?"

"Dierdra, what do you want me to say? I'm not angry. There's nothing wrong. I'm just tired. I'm going to bed. We can talk about things tomorrow."

"Carol, we haven't talked all week. I mean not like we did the first week. We were up every night talking. And then we had such a beautiful time out on the lake at

Echo Park, and then, suddenly, you seem to have disappeared from my life. What's happened?"

"I told you what happened. That new dishwashing machine that they got at Harmony House broke down, and they asked me to come and help out. I mean I'm working five hours a night. Now I'm tired and I'm going to sleep." Carol turned out the light, got undressed in the dark and got into bed. She heard Dierdra turn back, facing the wall, and the image burned her face and her chest and made her pull her legs up and wrap her arms around them as she had when she cannonballed into the lake. Then she must have sighed or made some sort of sound cause she heard Dierdra call, "Carol?" She didn't answer. She didn't dare answer.

CHAPTER SIX

Learning How to Seem

Orion thought that if she could withstand the pain of this grief without drinking or killing herself or killing someone else, she might somehow reach a point of clarity about how and why it all began, that she might pass through ordinary understanding to a way of knowing that would make all this clear, make it have meaning, let her see the beginning, the middle, let her have some hope that there would be a purpose in the end. She looked out at the Marble Mountains. "Does it ever stop?" she asked. Would there ever be a time she could say, 'Oh, it's like that,' and have some peace. Not be unconscious again, but have real peace.

She had been safely there, all those years with Frank and those years before that. But it was the safety of the coffin. Even in high school she knew that it wasn't really her smiling all the time, saying "Gee" and "Gosh" and dancing with her rump out in the air. Well, I learned how to seem, she told herself. But you never learned how to be. That's what I'm doing now. Being. You're no good at it. Then let me seem again.

Here Orion came to a full stop. Some gold leaves on the trail had stopped her. Aspen, maybe. The rain had probably brought them down. The wet leaves glistened. She bent down and scooped up a handful of loamy earth, one gold leaf in the center. This is the most beautiful mud pie I have ever seen, she thought. I did see beauty. I have seen it. I can, again. She brought the handful of earth closer and breathed in the damp dark smell of it. I know this. I know it deeper than I know anything.

She closed her eyes and felt herself move back to another time and place, across the mists and shimmers into the prickly dark roses of consciousness. She was right there on the lake at Echo Park.

                    *   *   *   *   *

Carol saw Denise and Dierdra through the glass door. They had shown up at the Harmony House at the same moment, nearly bumping into each other. Dierdra opened the door and allowed Denise to go in first. That kind of courtesy, Carol knew, came from someone who knew she would get her way in the end. Denise, on the other hand, was so folded in on her many losses, so sure she'd never get what she wanted that for a moment, Carol felt sorry for her. Here she came tight-lipped, frowning, to the back of the restaurant. Carol stood just inside the kitchen door, pretending to concentrate on the business of taking off her apron and putting on her sweater.

"What's she doing here?"

"How do I know?"

"You said we were doing something tonight. You spend all your time with her."

Dierdra had quickly joined them. "Hi. Hope I'm not being bothersome. Did you girls have something planned for tonight?"

Carol and Denise waited for the other to speak. Dierdra seized the moment. "Well, if it wasn't anything too definite, I need to talk to Carol about something important, something personal." Dierdra put her arm through Carol's and moved her toward the door.

Carol turned toward Denise. "I'll catch you later tonight. I promise."

"You promise?"

"I said."

Denise didn't say anything more, but she did push pass the two girls and stomp out the door ahead of them.

As soon as they were on the street, Dierdra smiled and said, "I have a confession to make."

"What?"

"I didn't really have anything important to tell you. I was fibbing. I just thought maybe we could go down to Echo Park and play ping pong. What do you think?"

"I'll beat you, you know!"

"No, you won't!"

Carol laughed, but she was thinking it was mean of Dierdra to lie like that, and Carol felt tricked somehow and then mean herself to just turn Denise away. Oh, well, she told herself, she'd been mean to Denise many times before. Why should this time be any different? It was different though, and arm and arm with

Dierdra, walking down Temple Street toward the park, a trip she'd made hundreds of times, Carol felt somehow she was not in familiar territory.

It felt odd at the ping pong table, too. She was suddenly aware of dings in the table surface and sags in the net that she'd never even noticed before, and she wasn't judging distances well, so that her serve was too hard or too soft, her returns too soon or too late.

"I don't know what's the matter with me, Dierdra. Guess I'm just too tired to play. Let's go rent a boat."

The sun was low, covering the bulrushes and the palm trees and the lake itself with a soft crimson light. The oars cut through the light and made it leap around the boat like big golden carp.

"Dierdra," Carol called, about to tell her friend how the sun was dancing in the water. But when she looked up, she saw the sun had set fire to Dierdra's hair, and she lost her breath for a second and then said, through the constrictions in her throat: "Your hair. It looks like it's on fire." She could have added that she'd never before seen the freckle on Dierdra's lip. She'd seen the ones on her nose and the ones sprinkled across her cheeks. But that one on her lip and that other one just below it on her chin—why she'd never seen them before.

She returned her gaze to the water, studied it, and felt the flames on her own face.

Dierdra stopped rowing, and in a tone so soft Carol could just hear her, she said, "Carol," and Carol looked up to see Dierdra sitting with her elbows on her knees, her long beautiful hands suspended in front of her. Dierdra leaned forward, and whispered again, "Carol."

"What?"

She looked straight into Carol's eyes, took a deep breath, and then, in the middle of it, changed course. She shook her head, let out a breathy laugh, looked out on the lake, shook her head again, and then looked back at Carol. "Nothing. I just thought it was time to change rowers." Then with a slight return to the voice and manner she'd had before, she said, "It's your turn." Dierdra reached her hands out so they could steady each other as they switched places. Carol took her hands and the girls rose and pulled closer to each other. Carol felt a current of heat flash through her body, down to her feet. Dierdra must have felt it too as they both, without a word, sat back down. Carol felt the current cross the space between their feet. She saw Dierdra's legs twitch, as though she had resisted clapping her knees together, and then they let go of each other and the current continued loose, charging the still night air between them.

Dierdra shivered. Then she grabbed up the oars and said, "I'm cold. Maybe we should go back in." Without waiting for Carol to say anything, she started rowing. Carol didn't know what to say anyway. They hardly spoke going back in, docking the boat, walking back up Temple Street, walking back to the Home. And in their room, which now seemed small, Dierdra muttered something about doing her homework and picked up one of her books. Carol opened a comic book.

After a few minutes Dierdra looked over her book at Carol and, with unexpected intensity, said, "Why do you read those silly comic books all the time?"

"Why not?"

"It's just a waste of time. You could at least do some sketches if you aren't going to study."

"I already told you I don't like to sketch when other people are around."

"Oh, Carol, you just waste your mind and your talents—"

"What do you care?"

"It's just a waste. That's all"

"Yeah. It's a waste. It's my choice, too. It's what I like to do, waste my time, waste myself. It's what I do best."

"I don't believe that."

Carol stood up. "Dierdra, I'm going out. I got to get something to eat."

"Where? Wait. I'll go with you."

Carol didn't want to say yes. She didn't want to say no, either. Then Dierdra reached for her socks. She had one foot on the floor and the other on the bed, and Carol could feel herself moving forward, spreading Dierdra's legs, further apart.

As if she could read Carol's thoughts, Dierdra suddenly looked up. "What is it? Why are you looking at me?"

"Your socks. Are those your socks? They look like mine."

"No they don't. You don't have socks like these." She looked hard at Carol and then said in a low whisper, "Your eyes were not on my socks, Carol."

Carol was frightened, caught. She punched her way out. "You know all the answers. Figure it out for yourself."

"Aren't you going to wait for me?"

"No."

"If you leave now, I won't be here when you get back. I'll call my parents to come and get me…for good."

"Go ahead. Call mommy and daddy."

"That's not fair."

Carol laughed.

"You just feel sorry for yourself." Dierdra hurled the words at Carol.

Carol didn't flinch. "You're wrong there. I don't feel anything at all, not for anyone." She reached into the pocket where she kept her tips and threw some change onto Dierdra's bed. "Call your folks. Get the hell out of here."

Dierdra was already at the door and through it before Carol had finished. She turned and said, "I'm a spoiled rich girl. I can call my parents collect."

Carol waited till she heard the phone being dialed. Then she walked down the hall, passing Dierdra, on her way to the stairs. She heard Dierdra saying, "Hi, Daddy," and she heard the exaggerated sweetness of it and was sure it was done for her benefit. She stopped, jerked the phone away from Dierdra and covered the receiver with her hand. Fixing her eyes straight onto Dierdra's, fixing her voice so it did not waver, she said, "Dierdra, you can't hurt me." Then she gave her one last hard look, handed the phone back to her and started down the stairs.

Carol walked down Temple Street to the Taqueria. She hadn't been there in a long time, not since she started working at the Harmony House after school. Mrs. Valle and half her kids ran the place. Federico, the oldest boy had already been in juvenile hall—he'd made a zip gun. They caught him because it exploded in his hand. "Well, what was he going to do with it?" everybody asked, meaning it didn't matter that he hadn't held anyone up yet. He would have. And maybe he'd have killed someone, too. So this punishment was a good thing, coming before the serious crime. Everyone said it would straighten him out, but Carol never saw anything crooked in Federico. He had a paper route in the morning, and he took care of the kids right after school and helped out a lot in the restaurant. Sometimes he did get into trouble at school all right, but it was just fights with other boys. He never talked back to his mother or teachers. He was no problem, none at all.

Sometimes when Carol would stop by to say hello and have a coke just before the Taqueria closed at ten o'clock, she'd find Federico standing at one end of the counter, trying to do his homework. For some reason, just seeing him like that would inspire Carol, and when she got back to the Home, she'd do her homework. She'd do it carefully, too, and the nuns would be surprised. Now and then they'd ask her who she copied it from. "Federico," she'd answer, though there was no Federico in her class.

When she visited him at juvie, he told her that he didn't want a gun; he wanted to see if he could put it together and make it work, just see if he could do it. He had put his head down then, and said more to himself than to Carol: "I don't know what I was trying to prove." Carol didn't know what to say, although she knew very well what he meant. She had the same strong urges to take risks and she suffered from a vague confusion over the things she did, but she continued, and knew that she would until something—outside herself—stopped her. And she wondered, like Federico, what she was trying to prove, and she felt curious and somehow fated to push through to some end and see where she was when she got there.

Carol and Federico had played together as children when Carol was living with Mrs. Martin, around the corner, on West-lake Avenue. Usually Carol was on the lookout, not wanting to run into Mrs. Martin, but tonight she didn't care one way or the other. There was hardly anyone on the street, though; just a few old guys sharing some wine, calling at her, one telling her to come back in five years, another telling her she should be home and not running around these streets. "I'm going home now. Don't you worry," Carol yelled back.

The bus pulled up and some old women got off, probably cleaning women coming in from Beverly Hills. Every one of them seemed to have bunions bursting through their shoes, and as they went seesawing by the old guys, Carol heard: "Evening ma'm." "Evening." The women answered, in just that one word, and in just the same way—as if there wasn't anything wrong in the whole world—"Evening." Something about the way they spoke to each other, didn't just walk by, but spoke kindly to each other, and even the way they called out to Carol, just playful, not letting her pass without saying something, expecting her to say something back—it all made her feel calmer.

The Taqueria was empty, except for Federico who was just standing there, no dishes, no broom or mop, nothing in his hands—just standing there as if he was waiting for her.

"Hey, Vato, que paso?" Carol yelled bursting through the door.

"El tren paso y no pito," Federico responded, not missing a beat, joy and welcome on his face, his arms already outstretched.

"I guess that train will never toot!" Carol said, moving happily into Federico's arms.

"I wish it would stop coming by."

They hugged for a long time. Then Federico said, "Oh, I missed these abrazos. Where have you been, chica?"

"I been working after school at the Harmony House. You know, down on Temple. Two new guys—white guys—bought it. They got lots a new stuff in there. It looks real different."

"You're looking kind of different yourself. What's up?"

"Nothing. Nothing. I'm hungry. Hey where is everybody?"

"Dinner rush is over. Dishes all washed and put up. Kids went home. So did Ma. Left me here to deal with the tough guys coming in late like you." Federico pretended to box with Carol, fading to the right and then to the left, and Carol pretended to get him with her left-right combination. "Mercy," he cried in a little boy's voice. "Just show me some mercy please!"

"Okay. If you have any enchiladas left."

"Chicken or cheese?"

"Both. I want both. And rice and beans. And a giant coke. Do you have any flan?"

"Andale!" Federico smiled and moved into action. "I'll get the food. You get the coke."

Just as Carol went behind the counter, she saw Mrs. Martin walk by the window, and Carol started to duck down, but caught herself. "I'm not scared of you," she said to that part of the wall where she figured Mrs. Martin was by then. She let her eyes move along to the next window and wait. Mrs. Martin showed up, actually glanced in the window but didn't seem to recognize the young woman standing behind the counter.

Probably drunk, Carol thought, and then she went around to the door and looked up the street after Mrs. Martin. She was walking her ratty little Chihuahua.

Carol went up to the pass-through window, and yelled into the kitchen. "Hey, Federico, I'm going to steal Mrs. Martin's dog. We can make a new dish: Chihuahua Enchilada!"

Federico laughed. "That dog's too mean to taste good."

"We could cover it with chocolate mole and give it to Mrs. Martin to eat."

"You still mad at her, chica?" Federico came through to the front holding Carol's dinner with a dishtowel. He placed it on the counter. "This is hot, you know."

"No, I don't let her bother me." Carol sat down and picked up her fork.

"You don't let nothing bother you."

"You do?"

"I'm a man."

"I wish I was a man," Carol said, earnestly stabbing into the rice and beans,

"Oyez, chica, don't say that. You're too cute and too nice to be a guy."

"I don't want to be cute or nice. I want to be strong."

"No one says you're not strong." Then Federico put his fists up in front of him. "But you just tell me who and I'll go beat them up. Okay?"

"Okay, I will," Carol smiled. "Can I have some more beans?"

Federico nodded and started back to the kitchen when the phone rang. Carol figured it was a long carry-out order cause Federico pointed into the kitchen for her to get her own beans, and then he started writing things down.

As she went into the kitchen and got her beans, and as she came back, sat down, and ate, Carol thought again of Mrs. Martin. Really, she knew it wasn't just Mrs. Martin. She'd had worse foster parents. It was that day, the last day with Mrs. Martin, the last time she saw Father John, that she didn't like to think about, and every time she saw Mrs. Martin, she'd remember it again. She moved back, in her mind, to a safer time, to those Fridays that Father John came to St. Teresa's to teach religion.

He was the first young priest Carol could ever remember

being in the parish, and he was handsome. Wavy black hair and warm brown eyes that had the kindest sweetest most understanding look in them she'd ever seen. And when he looked at her, she felt her whole body melt. Yet, somehow, she could find her voice and tell him anything—except how much she loved him. She tried to show him, though, by memorizing the entire Catechism.

*   *   *   *   *

Orion paused and tried to remember. "Why Did God Make Me?" She tested her memory. "He made me in his image...to testify?" She couldn't remember. But she remembered Father John very well. He was young and sweet and kind, maybe like Jesus. Not like God. God the Father. "To glorify Himself," she remembered.

It was Father John that introduced her to the mountains. He never took her there, of course, but he talked about them. The Sierras, the Trinity Alps, the Marble Mountains, on up into Oregon. Her child-ears heard Father John say it was the "Clammy Mountains" that he'd walked to, all the way in the next State, Oregon. She smiled when she realized it had to be these mountains, the Klamath, that he meant. And that she was in them. Lost. Maybe not lost. She'd found his mountains, hadn't she.

They were shrines to him. Cathedrals, he said. Places people could find peace, even if they couldn't find it anywhere else. We'll see, she said, with her usual sense of cynicism, which was quickly accompanied by an unfamiliar touch of possibility.

It started to rain, a soft rain, accompanied by a gusting wind. Orion had come to the bottom of a trail that took her into some Manzanita bushes. She turned to get her bearings, but the mountain she'd descended was not behind her. Ahead, everything was dark, gray, vague, and the rain was beginning to ice up. It's going to hail, she told herself, and immediately she felt herself being pelted by it. The only thing she could make out, beyond the Manzanita, was another mountain—or maybe it was the one she'd just come down. She couldn't be sure. "Oh, Jesus," she sighed. "If I make it, okay. If I don't make it, okay." She took off through the Manzanita, going toward the mountain, and she wished like hell she'd brought some brandy.

$$*\qquad*\qquad*\qquad*\qquad*$$

Carol had been living with Mrs. Martin for three years, since Fourth Grade, and she was trying to learn to wake up without using an alarm clock because the alarm would wake Mrs. Martin, and Mrs. Martin didn't like being awakened at all by anyone.

This particular morning, Carol didn't manage to wake up till a quarter to nine. School started in fifteen minutes. Carol found the shorts and T-shirt she'd had on the night before, and was dressed and out the door in two minutes. She ran across the street to the cleaners, but there was a sign up saying they wouldn't be back till ten-thirty. She had to decide whether to go to school without her uniform, or wait till the cleaners opened and then try to sneak into school during recess, or what she finally decided: to try to salvage her other uniform.

When she got back home, Mrs. Martin was in the kitchen, looking for something in the refrigerator. The dog was yapping for food and running back and forth, tapping its nervous little feet upon the linoleum.

"Is the baby hungry? Yes, I know the baby's hungry, but first mommy has to have some juice." Mrs. Martin caught Carol as she passed the kitchen. "Hey, where's the goddamn orange juice? Why aren't you in school? Isn't this Monday?"

"The cleaners is closed."

"So wear your other uniform."

"It's dirty."

Mrs. Martin continued her search for the juice, but added a sort of half-hearted, "You know you ought to plan things better." Carol started to go back to the bedroom. "Goddamnit it. Did you finish all the juice?"

"No. I didn't have any."

"You're lying."

"I got to go get dressed. I didn't drink it. I don't even like it." Carol ran into the bedroom. She was frantic not to be late again, but she was already late and she had so many detentions for being tardy and so many detentions for not wearing her uniform. And she'd run out of lies and even out of truths that the nuns would accept. Christ! She set up the ironing board and found the iron. Her uniform was on the closet floor, along with everything else that should have been on a hanger or in a drawer. She ran to the bathroom where she'd washed and hung her blouse the night before; it was still damp, but she could iron it dry.

"Carol, you're a goddamn liar," Mrs. Martin met her in the hallway between the bathroom and bedroom. "There's no goddamn juice in that refrigerator and I know goddamn well there was some there when I left last night. Are you paying attention?"

"I got to iron this blouse."

"I'll tell you what you got to do. You got to get me some

orange juice to replace the orange juice you drank some time between when I left last night and when I got up this morning."

"It's after nine."

"Then it's already late and it don't matter if you're two more minutes late. I'll iron the blouse. Go."

"I need some money."

"Charge it at the chink's."

"He won't let me anymore."

"Don't you sass me. Go get me that juice. Tell the chink I'll pay him on Friday. Give me that blouse." She snatched it from Carol's hand.

Carol couldn't think of anything else to do but go up to the store and get the juice and hope Mrs. Martin wouldn't burn her blouse. She ran out of the house and ran past the Chinese store—no hope in her heart that he'd let her charge it—up to the big store another block over and stole some frozen orange juice. She passed the cleaners both ways. It was still closed.

When she got home, she rushed into the kitchen and turned the hot water tap on, put the container of juice in a pan, and rushed into the bedroom. Mrs. Martin was pressing the iron onto Carol's blouse, finishing the collar, but as soon as she saw Carol, she started talking and stopped moving the iron.

"Did you get it?"

"Yeah. It's thawing."

"Christ. That'll take forever. It's expensive, too. How much was it?"

"Here, let me do it," Carol said, trying to take the iron away.

"I asked you a question," Mrs. Martin stated, pressing the iron more firmly upon the blouse.

"I stole it."

Mrs. Martin lifted the iron from the blouse, as if to hit Carol with it. Carol was relieved.

"What did you say?"

"I didn't have time to argue with the chink."

Mrs. Martin set the iron down, reached across the board, and slapped Carol hard across the face. Carol seized the opportunity and picked up the iron and started pressing her blouse from her side of the board.

"Where are you learning that stuff? I never taught you to steal." Mrs. Martin moved toward the kitchen, her thirst stronger than her anger. "Don't you ever steal nothing again. Do you hear me?"

Carol heard her stomping into the kitchen and then yelling again: "What are you trying to do in here? Don't you know hot water costs money? Where am I going to get the money for all the goddamn water you use? You think you're the Queen of Sheba, but you're not. You don't have to work for a living. You think you can steal your way through life. Well you can't. You got to pay and pay and pay and pay. Do you hear me!"

"Yes, Mrs. Martin. I hear you."

"What did you say?"

"I said I heard you."

"Don't you answer me with that tone of voice!"

"Yes, ma'm." Carol finished her blouse and held it up for inspection. Mrs. Martin had scorched the collar. It would show. Carol rummaged through the drawers looking for the chalk she used for hopscotch. She found it and quickly ran it across the scorched places on her collar. Then she ironed her very soiled skirt. She could smell the dog. He'd been sleeping on it. She sprinkled some of Mrs. Martin's perfume over it and tried to iron it in. Then she put on her socks and shoes. Her shoes were a mess. She grabbed the Dine Shine and quickly went over the shoes, still wearing them. She got some of the brown polish on her socks, but she didn't have time to change or do anything but get out of there.

She looked up the first alley—there were three of them that led to the school—and she saw Rufus and Fanny sitting on the old couch the winos shared. Fanny called out to her: "Hi, there, hon. Going to school?"

"Yeah. I'm late."

"Well you better go on. Them nuns is waiting on you."

Rufus hardly ever said anything unless he was so drunk he was raving. When that happened he usually took all his clothes off and made terrible scenes. Mrs. Martin had called the police on him before, once when she was drunk too, and the police had almost taken them both off. Carol smiled to herself, continuing her sprint up the alley, across the street, and on up the next two alleys to school.

The church bells rang ten o'clock as Carol entered the building, like a thief. There was no one in the hallway; just the dark oil paintings of the saints pierced with arrows and the sinners licked by the flames of hell. Carol ran her hands through her hair. It was sticking up all over, she knew, thick and frizzy. Mrs. Martin called it Brillo. Carol took the three flights of stairs. She stopped for a moment in front of the gray, eyeless statue of Mary.

Then she ran a last hopeless hand through her hair and stood in front of the door to the classroom, trying to get up the courage to go in.

The door opened before her and Sister Mary Joan was upon her. "I saw you running up the street, Carol. You came from the alley, didn't you? I have already spoken to you and to Mrs. Martin about those alleys. They are dangerous. It was just lucky I happened to glance out the window and saw you. It is time you learned to face a few things, young lady."

Carol stood there waiting for what she would learn.

CHAPTER SEVEN

A Sin of Thought

Orion stopped, took off her backpack, and held it over her head. The hail cracked down on her head. The hail cracked down on her shoulders and hands. 'You got to pay and pay and pay and pay.' It was Mrs. Martin's voice. I should be punished for all this bounty? Despair is a sin, the worst sin. I am committing the worst sin, so I'll go to hell. What could I ever do to deserve to be set in flames and burned forever? I could kill them both. Even then, forever? Two hours. Maybe two weeks.

She continued walking, dismissing the idea of burning in hell. The hail and this life seemed sufficient. She damned the Church and all it's helpers, the black nuns and blacker priests, pink-jowled and scrubbed, intervening, not letting her find God at all. She was lost in every way. Maybe she'd die in the Clammy Mountains.

"Don't worry, Father John. I am not feeling despair. Not at

the moment, anyhow." In fact, the hail crashing down on her was lifting her up, bringing her back to life. She could die there, of course, but that would not be despair. That would be having no compass, having no trail to speak of, and having not much care about where she ended up. But, yes, she did want to end up somewhere. . .alive. "Oh, Father, dear Father," she said aloud as she now began pushing her way through the slashing branches of Manzanita, "please show me the way."

*   *   *   *   *

Sister Mary Joan and Carol were standing in the doorway, separated from the class by the cloakroom, but Carol was sure everyone could hear. She was afraid to tell a lie, afraid the students would laugh cause they'd know she was lying, but she didn't want to just stand there and wait. Finally, she opened her mouth to say something—she didn't know what—but Sister Mary Joan stopped her with, "Is that perfume? Are you wearing perfume?"

It was an awful smell—Mrs. Martin's perfume ironed into her cotton-wool skirt, into the dank smell left on her skirt by Mrs. Martin's dog.

Carol wanted to run, but she knew they'd expel her for sure and then she didn't know where they'd send her. So she stood there, reeking, her mind racing through lies and truths and possibilities of punishment, weighing what to do with what might be done to her, about the rules of dress and conduct. Then she came to an end. Carol looked up. "Do you have anything to say for yourself, young lady?"

"No, sister."

"Good. Come in." Carol did as she was told, the whole class looking at her and, she thought, smelling her.

After she had taken her seat, Sister Mary Joan announced that they were doing Inspection. They had just finished Inspection of Deed. Inspection of Thought was next, and after that there would be Inspection of Books and Desks. At the end Inspection of Uniforms. Then, the nun looked directly at Carol: "Because you were late, Carol, you will have to combine Deed and Thought. I hope you will be especially conscientious in examining both Deed and Thought."

"Yes, sister."

Carol waited for the Inspection of Thought to begin, hoping she could reach into her desk and find the chalk they were given to whiten the bindings of their books; she needed to go over her collar again.

"Inspection of Thought." Carol looked out of the corner of her downcast eyes. Sister Mary Joan's eyes, which were also supposed to be downcast, were still on Carol.

The students joined in as Sister Mary Joan began: "A sin of thought is as grievous as a sin of deed."

Then by herself the nun asked: "Have we had any bad thoughts since our last Inspection?" Carol wondered to herself if she'd had anything else. Then Sister Mary Joan led them through the Ten Commandments while Carol looked out of the corner of her downcast eyes for a chance to run the chalk over the collar of her blouse again. It was not until "Thou shalt not kill" that Sister Mary Joan finally closed her eyes.

Carol passed Book and Desk Inspection, but even before it started, she knew she'd never make it through Uniform. Sister Mary Joan walked up and down the rows of children who stood like little soldiers, bearing up under her quick sharp glances. There was an unbuttoned shirt here, an untied shoelace there, but everyone knew this particular inspection was being done because of Carol. When the nun finally reached her—Carol was in the Sinking Ship row—she came to an abrupt halt, causing the beads on her rosary and the crucifix and the length of stiff leather that hung from the nun's belt to clatter like chains.

"What is that odor?"

"It's mostly the perfume."

"Does perfume please God?"

"No, sister."

"Then we will go and wash it off."

"Yes, sister." Carol started to move toward the door.

"Not so fast, young lady."

Carol returned to her desk.

"What have you done to your blouse?"

"Mrs. Martin burned it."

"Who burned it?"

"I burned it."

"That's better."

"Are those holes in your socks?"

"No sister. It's Dine Shine."

"Did you ever think to shine your shoes before you put them on?"

"Yes, sister."

"Well?"

"I was late—"

"Carol, you are often late. I must say, though, I don't think I've ever seen you in quite such disarray. This is most unfortunate because the Head of our Order is going to be here this afternoon, and she might well visit this class. I do not want her to find you like this in my class." She paused. "Need I remind you that the school supplied you your uniforms? None of the other children have been shown so much privilege, but you… you…you must go home and change. Be back here before recess ends." She looked hard at the girl. "That gives you one full hour. Do not be late. Do you understand?"

Carol was trembling with embarrassment, but still, she saw a break in her bad luck. The cleaners would be open. She could change her socks and comb her hair. "Yes, sister. Thank you, sister."

She ran home. Mrs. Martin had gone to work. Carol washed her other blouse first and hung it in a window to dry. Then she ran over to the cleaners. The door was locked, and she could see through the window on the wall clock that it was past ten-thirty. It was nearly ten forty-five, but there was no one there, and the same sign was hanging in the window.

Carol banged on the door, desperate that someone be in there. When she lost hope, she banged harder. Hot tears rushed down her face, and she started kicking at the door. Finally, she started banging the door with her head, and she knew she was having one of her fits, but she didn't want to stop, and she didn't stop until she came up with a plan that would take her all the way to crazy. She would show herself to whomever it was Sister Mary Joan was so worried about, and she would give them something to look at.

She ran past her house and started up the alley. Fanny and Rufus were right where she'd seen them last. Carol sat down on the ground across from their burnt out fire pit and asked them for a drink. They'd given her sips before, and now Fanny held out her bottle saying, "You sure do look upset, child. What's bothering you all the time?"

"Nothing. I just get crazy. I'm crazy right now. I'm having a fit." Carol drank deeply and, for a second, thought it might all come back up.

"Where's the fit you having? I don't see it. Do you, Rufus?" Rufus, of course, said nothing at all.

"It starts like this," Carol held out her hands. She'd broken some blood vessels banging on the door. "I just get crazy. I went to the cleaners. I have to have my uniform. They're closed. They're supposed to be open. Things like that make me crazy, so I started banging on the door and kicking it and then I hurt my head banging it on the door. Ain't that crazy?"

"Well, they ain't going to open any sooner if you bang on the door with your head stead of your hands. That's for sure!" Fanny laughed. "Here," she said, handing the bottle back to Carol. "Sit for a spell longer. They bound to open soon."

Carol took the bottle. "No, I can't. I have to go back to school." Then she took another deep swig and gave the bottle back to Fanny. This time there was no trouble keeping it down. All she felt was warmth and comfort. She stood up; already her knees felt weak and her heart a little bit stronger. "Thanks, Fanny."

"Well, you owe me."

"Okay. See you. Bye, Rufus."

Carol started up the alley and stumbled on something, a rock maybe. It gave her a start on how to carry on now with this fit she was having. She fell to the ground and started rolling, rolling up the alley, against gravity. She could feel the grit and gravel and broken glass under her, but it was all going too slowly, so she stopped, and then surrendered to the downward pull which took her back to the bottom where Fanny and Rufus sat watching.

"I see you having a fit all right," Fanny laughed.

Rufus seemed to come to life. He held out his bottle to her. It surprised Carol. She got up and went over and took it from him. "Thank you, Rufus." She wasn't sure, but maybe he smiled. Then he looked away. She raised the bottle to her mouth and sipped, knowing she'd have no trouble now keeping it down, knowing it would taste good. She took two long swigs. Rufus didn't protest, but Fanny said: "Whoa, child, if you want to get back to school. Anyway, that's all Rufus has for the day. Be sure and pay him back, hear?"

"I will."

"You better go now, though I don't know they going to let you in looking like that." Fanny laughed again. "This how you look when you have a fit?"

Carol nodded.

"Well, that's better than Rufus look when he do."

Carol laughed cause that was the truth. One more sip, not too long, and she handed the bottle back to him. "I'll pay you back. Thank you."

Carol kept Rufus in her mind as she headed back up the alley. Rufus, naked, shouting about the war. They said he had a steel plate in his head. They joked that he won it in the war, like an award. And sometimes he did put his uniform on, or just the shirt with the medals he had won still on it, and he would try to take down the billboards on Sunset Boulevard. The police would come and take him away and you wouldn't see him for a long time. Then he'd show up again quiet, clean dark clothes on. But it wouldn't be long before he was at it again, crazier than before. And it was at his craziest, naked, wearing a helmet, way up onto the rafters of the Lucky Strike billboard, bayoneting the man in the suit smoking the cigarette that Carol saw Rufus in her mind as she ran up the alley, and she took every bit of that craziness and stuffed it into her small fit, to make it bigger, to make the whole thing burst.

She started running into things, crashing into anything she could along the alleyways—the scrubby bushes, the trashcans, the abandoned cars. She caught her blouse on something and it ripped down the front. She tried to rip her skirt herself, but it was too thick and it frustrated her so she started slapping herself to punish herself for being so helpless and weak. But those slaps started to calm her down, so she stopped and then she saw she was in front of the school. "Okay," she said, "I hope you're ready."

It was almost time for lunch. Carol could hear the class reciting their prayers. She imagined Sister Mary Joan and whoever-it-was watching the good little children saying their prayers. She ruffled her hair to make it wilder, saw there was blood on her hands, wiped them on her shirt and skirt and burst through the school door, up the stairs and through the door to her classroom. But even before she passed the cloakroom, she realized something was wrong.

Sister Mary Joan wasn't there. The students were there, eyes wide upon her. But Sister Mary Joan wasn't there. There wasn't any nun there. It was a priest.

"My God!" Carol screamed, and then she ran from the room. She could hear someone coming after her down the hall. She ran faster, but he caught her and tried to turn her around, but Carol started punching at him. The priest hugged her to him, stopping her fists, stopping her fit.

"Carol, what's happened to you?"

She had kept her eyes closed during the tussle, hoping against hope that it wasn't who she thought it was holding her now. Hoping at the same time that it was. Very softly she said, "Father John?"

"Yes, Carol?"

"Oh, no," she cried, and then she buried her head in his chest, feeling she might die from shame.

Father John picked her up, and Carol felt herself go limp, heard herself burst into tears. He carried her down stairs and into the playground and sat them both down on a bench, Carol weeping uncontrollably into his sacred vestments. She had no words. She didn't want to tell him the truth, but she couldn't lie to Father John. There weren't any words, anyway, that she could think of that could explain how she felt or why she felt like this. She cried and he held her, and she knew somehow that this was some kind of truth.

*   *   *   *   *

"Carol," Federico touched her arm, and she jumped. He was standing next to her. "Something wrong, chica?"

Carol brushed the tears from her eyes. "Yeah, but I don't know what. Just things. You know what I mean?"

"Yeah, I know," he said, and she knew he did.

Carol called Denise from the Taqueria.

"I didn't think you'd call."

"I'm calling. Do you want to go out or not?"

"Yeah. Let's go down to the park and see if any of those cute guys from Baby Temple are there."

"No. I don't want to go to the park. Let's go to Virgil or Belmont—see if there's a dance."

"I don't have nothing to wear."

"We'll steal something."

"We don't have time. Where were you anyway?"

"Denise, I'm at the Taqueria. In thirty minutes I'm leaving, and I'm going to a dance. Do you want to come with me?"

"Yeah."

"Well come on then."

Federico told the girls he knew there was a dance at Belmont for sure. It cost more to go to the high school dances, but they were bigger than the junior high dances, and sometimes they had live music, so the girls decided to spend the money.

The music was live that night. When the girls walked into the gym, the band was playing "Night Train," and the guy playing the sax sounded just like Earl Bostic.

"He's really cool looking," Denise said to Carol.

"He's cute," she agreed. "The drummer's cute, too."

"Not as cute as the saxophone player."

"I wonder if any of the West Temple girls are here." Carol looked around, but didn't see any of them. She did see Sleepy Sam, though, and he saw her at about the same moment. He smiled a shy smile, biting his lower lip, and started across the room toward her, slow and very cool. It wasn't his slowness that got him the nickname, though. It was his eyes. Even when he got excited about something, his eyes just didn't seem to open all the way. Denise said it wasn't his eyes, it was because he never said anything and that put everyone to sleep. That was why they called him that.

Sleepy Sam reached for Carol's hand without a word. She gave it to him without a word, and then followed behind him as he made way for them to get onto the dance floor.

They didn't move to every beat or every other beat. They were doing the Fish. Their feet weren't going to be moving. Everything else was. And they wouldn't move that everything-else till it felt right. Carol listened to the saxophone, listened to the silent signals from Sleepy Sam, heard no thoughts in her head, no howls in her heart. She swayed when he swayed, stayed when he stayed. They were doing the Fish—safe, warm, held.

The music ended with one large blast of the saxophone. Then he shifted into the slow strong surge of Harlem Nocturne, the saxophone holding the first few notes open till they crested and then letting it all fall with a sigh. Just to have something to say about it, Sleepy Sam and Carol decided on a counter rhythm, still holding on to each other but moving faster than before to this slower music, double-timing the music, enjoying their private understanding. And Carol heard Sleepy Sam say "umm," and that involuntary pushed out sound filled her body with light, so much light there was no room for shadow.

*   *   *   *   *

Frank's silence was nothing like that. It kept her out, away, unknown, in the dark. Why must she think of him? "Oh, Father, dear Father, please show me the way," she chanted again, and then added, "The life of a martyr today is so gray."

Well, what was she supposed to have done? Loved him for all the things he didn't do? That's what the therapist seemed to imply. "He doesn't drink too much or gamble too much; he doesn't chase after women or stay out late. He's a good provider. What do you want?" But the time came and she needed help. He couldn't just not be bad. It was a sin of omission. A greater sin than murder. Willfully not helping someone you love. That should send you to hell for a few weeks. He not only didn't help. He ran. Ran to his cheerleader who knew he was married and didn't care at all. Siss boom bahed her way into my home. Rah rah rahed me right out the door. How did I let her get away with it?

Suddenly Orion stood, stretched her arms to the sky, and yelled, "Give me an R! Give me an A! Give me an H!" And she thought she could kill them both.

As she headed up the mountainside, Orion asked herself if even now in all this pain she would be willing to trade what she was beginning to understand for safety, for the safety of what seemed like love, of what was some sort of protection. Now, no protection, no room at the table. Now further into the shadows.

Or, if she went further still, could she learn to see in the dark? Could she find a different light?

Orion was frightened. She had been frightened so much of her life. Yet, she could remember that there was a time when she didn't seem to be afraid of anything. What had happened? Maybe it was that table, seeing it well lit, laden. She had always been hungry.

Brigid had said something about ninety percent of the people living in poverty were women and children, most of them white. They don't belong. Disqualified. 'Jesus,' Orion said to herself, 'I don't want to be on the outside looking in again. What if I turned back? Eased back in? Filled my eyes with adoration.

Filled my heart with praise. Smiled, grateful to the man who would then hold my chair out for me? But he wouldn't have me now.'

Orion left the thought, returned to her rhyme, and within a few miles had some lines she was pleased with: "Oh, Father, dear Father, please show me the way. The life of a martyr today is so gray. The fire is neon. The passion is gas. I'm turning just me on. I ask for the mass."

She walked, as devoid of thought as she could manage, for the rest of the afternoon, and sometime during those blank hours, two more lines came to her, and she knew the poem was finished: "It hurts too much, but not enough."

It was early evening when she caught, faintly at first, the pungent aroma of burning wood. It wafted down to her, increasing in potency, with the wind that was heading for the valley floor. Orion was surprised, but the thought of another living being and a warm campfire interested her. She walked toward the fire.

*   *   *   *   *

Carol and Denise got back to the Home just before door-lock. They'd stayed at the dance till midnight. Sleepy Sam walked them home. When they got to the door, Denise ran inside and Sleepy Sam gave Carol a friendly goodnight kiss. If it weren't so late, Carol thought, I'd change this kiss. Her thought must have registered somewhere between them because Sleepy Sam gently held her away from him, looked into her eyes, a smile in his half-closed eyes, and said, "Hey, what's up with you?"

At the same moment, Denise yelled: "Carol! You're going

to be locked out."

"I'll take the window."

"Sister Mary Gregory's coming right now. She's already seen you."

"Okay. I'm sorry. I'd like to stay."

"You know what I'd like to do? Take you home. Give you some pan dulce and Mexican chocolate. Sleep together. I mean sleep."

"Why?"

"That's the way you feel tonight."

"How do I feel other nights?"

"It's different. Every time it's different."

"Carol! Here she comes!"

"Thanks Sleepy. I'll see you next time. Really, thanks."

"Hasta proxima."

"Hasta proxima."

Carol didn't know it, of course, but there wouldn't be a next time. If she knew, she might have turned and run back to Sleepy, gone home with him. Or maybe knowing wouldn't have made any difference to her at all.

Sister Mary Gregory was holding the door open and clearing her throat. Carol went past her saying, "Good evening, Sister."

"Good evening, Carol. I'm glad you're on time."

Carol looked to see if she was being sarcastic. She wasn't.

"Thank you, Sister."

Denise was waiting for her on the stairs. "Why'd you take so long? What were you talking about? I didn't think he could talk!"

The girls started up the stairs, Carol smiling. "Food. We were talking about food."

"He kissed you, didn't he?"

"We always kiss goodnight."

"Yeah, but not like that."

"You were watching us!"

"Not exactly."

"Then you don't know. Anyway, it's none of your business."

"Hey, I'm just talking."

"You know you talk too much."

"Oh, yeah, guess I should be deaf and dumb like Sleepy Sam."

"I tell you what: You could be silent for ten years and not know half of what he knows about people."

"Oh, Carol, that doesn't even make sense."

Carol sighed. "Maybe not. Maybe I'm crazy. Anyway, I'm tired. See you tomorrow."

"I noticed Dierdra didn't go home for the weekend."

"She didn't?"

"Don't tell me you didn't know."

"I didn't know, Denise, and I don't care."

"Oh, yeah, well you look interested enough."

"How do you know anyway? How do you always know everybody's business?"

"Cause I keep my eyes and ears open. And when you called me tonight, she came running out to the phone like it had to be for her. And I think she was listening from her room the whole time we were talking. Now why do you suppose she'd care about who I was talking to unless she thought it was you?"

"She probably wasn't even listening. Not everyone is as nosy as you are."

They reached the top of the stairs, said goodnight, and went

into their rooms. Dierdra was there all right, and from the look
of things she'd meant to stay awake. The lights were on, books
were scattered all over her bed, and there was a pen in her hand.
But she was asleep, facing the wall, the blankets well around
her this time, dark red curls covering most of her face. Carol
couldn't decide whether she was happy or not that Dierdra was
there, and she couldn't decide whether to make a lot of noise
and wake her up or just let her sleep. Sleep, she thought. That's
what I want. A long, long sleep. Not wanting water or brush to
wake Dierdra, Carol put some toothpaste on her finger, rubbed
it onto her teeth, and swallowed. Then she changed into her
pajamas, turned out the lights, crawled into bed, and fell into
a deep sleep.

*   *   *   *   *

The sun was bright as Orion entered the clearing. There was no
one around, but there were signs of life: a backpack with a tarp
over it, some jeans draped over the tarp, cooking equipment.
The fire was nearly out.

Orion loosened the straps on her backpack and let it drop
behind her. She took a long branch and stirred the live coals,
adding some tinder from a nearby pile of wood. She was soaked
with sweat, and her clothes were still wet from the rain. She took
her things off, propping her boots up near the fire, and then she
wrung out her socks and the rest of her clothes and laid them
haphazardly on the Manzanita that stood sparsely, now innocu-
ously, a few feet away. When she pulled her pack in closer to the
fire, she saw there was a rend in the bottom compartment. All
her food and the water bottle had fallen out. "Idiot! Imbecile!

Lunatic!" she screamed, and she slapped herself hard across her face. Then she took a breath. "Stop," she said suddenly, but softly. "Stop," she said and patted her chest just over her heart. Then she heard herself say, "It's all right. I'm here. It's all right." She didn't know where the inspiration had come from, but she noted that the words and the movement made her feel calmer.

After a moment, she looked around the camp to see if there might be some water, but she didn't see any. No food either. She'd just wait. She dug into the upper compartment of her pack and pulled out some shorts and a shirt and put them on. Then she took her tarp and spread it out near the fire, put her sleeping bag down on top of the tarp, and then let herself fall prostrate upon the ground, the sleeping bag cushioning her against the cold hard earth.

CHAPTER EIGHT

A Sin of Deed

She couldn't say exactly when it was she became aware that someone—Dierdra—was breathing on her shoulder. She didn't open her eyes and didn't move, but somehow Dierdra knew that Carol had finally felt her presence.

"Don't be angry."

Carol was silent.

"Carol? Are you angry?"

Carol felt her own heart racing, and she felt Dierdra's heart racing too, beating against her back as if she had two hearts or as if the two of them had one body.

"I know you're awake. I know you know I'm here with you."

Without speaking Carol turned to face Dierdra and when she did, she put her hand on Dierdra's shoulder, holding her away as Sleepy Sam had held her away. There was some light coming from the street, but it was so faint Carol could just make out Dierdra's features. She felt the warmth of her body, though, and smelled it, too.

"What is it?"

"You know. I know you know."

"I know. But I don't know either."

She felt Dierdra's body relax a little.

"Carol, I'm in love with you."

A flash of heat slapped Carol's cheeks, and she was suddenly aware of the small hairs on the back of her neck and along her arms. Again her heart raced. She felt her throat tighten.

"And I know you love me, too. I know you do."

Carol couldn't speak.

"And I know you want to kiss me." She tried to move closer, but Carol's hand still kept her at a distance.

"Let me come closer."

Carol couldn't think where she could put her hand if she moved it away from Dierdra's shoulder, but Dierdra didn't wait any longer. She took Carol's hand and put it on her breast and moved her closer to Dierdra.

"Feel my heart?"

"Yes."

"I'm full of love for you." Dierdra's voice had turned into a whisper and ran across Carol's hearing like wind itself, the words "feel" and "full" soughing across her ears, blowing into her breasts, flowing down into her hips.

"Dierdra," she managed. She had stopped herself from saying that she was afraid.

"Kiss me," Dierdra whispered.

Carol felt the bed, the room, her whole world, turn and dip and turn again and rise as she tried to pass through what she knew was forbidden to what she knew she had to have. She felt heavy, weighted, buried in sand.

"Come closer, Carol."

"I can't move," she said, but saying it gave her strength and she moved closer, and as she did, Dierdra licked her lips and Carol's world stopped turning. There was no world, there were only those lips wet and open.

"I'm going to kiss you," she said foolishly, some part of her still unbelieving, some part of her fearing this was a bluff, that she was being tricked, that this could not be happening.

Dierdra put her arm around Carol's shoulder and gently pulled her across. Their lips brushed each other awkwardly. Then Dierdra surprised Carol by rolling over on top of her and whispering, "Open your mouth just a little." And when Carol had opened her mouth just a little, Dierdra licked Carol's lips and then she flicked her tongue against Carol's tongue and pressed her mouth against her lips so gently, so sweetly, Carol heard herself moan. Dierdra went more deeply this time, into the moan, quieting it, and Carol was surprised at the heat and fullness of Dierdra's tongue; it tasted foreign, and it was shocking, and it set her on fire.

*　　　*　　　*　　　*　　　*

"How was your game?" Orion asked across the dinner table.

"Okay." Frank looked up from the paper. "How was your day with the convicts?"

Orion hesitated, but then she thought she might try: "I had one of the best days of my life."

"That's nice. I told you it's nice out on the golf course."

"Well, you're right. It's beautiful. I enjoyed myself. I enjoyed the other people."

"Right," he said, assuming she was kidding.

Orion pressed on. "First, I went with another woman up to the top of the hill there just off the golf course where the pine trees are really thick." She looked to see if he was still listening. He seemed to be. "There's a colony of rabbits up there." He seemed to be. He was listening, but he was waiting for the point. "I'd never seen a rabbit colony before." He was going back to the paper. "They're very funny, the way they stop and start. Most of them freeze and then just a couple of them hop any sort of way…." She began to feel foolish. "It was fun," she said and let it go.

"That's nice," he said into the paper.

Orion got up from the table. "Would you like another drink?"

"Make it a scotch, this time," he said.

Orion went into the kitchen and poured nine jiggers of gin into a glass pitcher. She poured one jigger of vermouth in after it. Then she placed the pitcher in a bowl of crushed ice, and with a thick glass wand, stirred the mixture for sixty seconds. She went to the refrigerator, opened the freezer door. Her martini glasses, three of them, stood in a row, faintly frosted. She took a jumbo green olive with a pimiento at its center, and dropped it into one of the glasses. Then she went back to the kitchen counter poured herself a martini and took one sip which she swished around in her mouth before she swallowed it. One more swallow and the martini was gone. She put some ice in a whiskey glass, poured straight scotch into it, poured herself another martini and took the drinks back to the table.

"Are you through with your plate?"

Frank nodded, not looking up from the paper.

"Here's your drink."

"Thanks, honey."

Orion cleared the table, had another drink in the kitchen, then came back and sipped the drink she'd left on the table. She looked out the window. The view was dim and gray except for the stand of Eucalyptus across the way. The camel colors of the bark and the khaki green of the leaves turned brighter under the soft rain. This time, as she looked at them, they looked like a gathering of women, turning to hear each other, bending to say things, the leafy branches falling around their bodies like tresses, open, free, intimate.

"I'm going to sketch for awhile."

"Okay."

At roll call the next morning, Brigid hardly acknowledged Orion. A quick smile. That was all. The policewoman had already told Orion that she'd have her own cart, and Orion wondered if Brigid had arranged that. Then she thought she was simply flattering herself, dismissed the idea and stood in the cold early morning to answer roll call.

Mary was late, came running in just after her name was called, hair stuck out to the sides, sitting on her head like a roof of straw.

"I said 'Here' from over there. I heard you call my name. Didn't you hear me answer? I said 'Here.'"

The policewoman shook her head, her rueful smile not just for Mary but for all of them to see. "This is what happens. I don't want to send you down to the Branch, Mary. But I don't see just what else I can do, do you?"

"Toilet duty."

"You already done that, everybody knows."

"Excuse me, ma'm," Captain Cushman spoke up. The policewoman looked his way. She was listening.

"The lunchroom looks like it could use a good cleaning and mopping. All the tables need to be swabbed down, too, and the kitchen area…."

"Mary?"

"I can do it!"

"And toilet duty."

"Thank you, ma'am."

Mary had broken out into a sweat, in spite of the cold. She wasn't wearing a jacket, either. After the group was dismissed, Captain Cushman offered Mary his jacket, but she was ready to go to work, focused on that one thing, and seemed to be refusing the interruption more than the jacket itself. She raised her hands, as if deflecting a blow, and then took off at a trot to the supply room.

Captain Cushman smiled, turned to the rest of them and said, "That's going to be one clean kitchen we hit today!"

Orion had noticed, the day before at final roll call, that some of the men had brought out their collection of golf balls and counted them in front of each other. The man with the most was, apparently, a long-running inmate and a long-running champion. They called him Top Flite by way of acknowledgment. When he showed up drunk—or half-drunk, as he liked to put it—they called him Full Flite. He didn't mind just as long as they didn't say it too loudly. He didn't want to be sent down to the Branch.

This morning, Top Flite was challenged by a newcomer, a

man who'd started his time at Pacific Pines with Carol. He was young and mean looking, a permanent snarl on his face and greasy brown hair down on his eyes.

"Top Flight, I'm going to find more golf balls today than you ever dreamed of."

"Okay, youngster. You go ahead. But you won't beat old Top-Flite."

"I will, old man, I will too."

Orion felt a sudden fear for Top Flite, afraid he might lose his title to this new fellow. She looked around for Brigid, thinking they could pick up some extra golf balls for the old guy and throw them into his bag when he wasn't looking, but Brigid was nowhere in sight.

Orion started up her cart and took off for the rabbit prairie driving the path Brigid had taken the day before, taking the steepness in stride, liking it, hoping Brigid would be there. She wasn't. Orion waited, watched the rabbits for a few minutes, and then went back down the hill. She found a good place to rake leaves somewhere on the back nine, and went to work, concentrating on the shapes and color of the dew-wet leaves, stopping only for a moment at a time to admire her progress, filling bag after bag, tying the pull cords into bows, tossing the bags into the back of the cart until there was no more room, driving the cart to the dumpster, and climbing the three-step ladder that gave her easy clearance to throw the bags in.

Orion wasn't sure if it was her fourth or fifth trip back, but she'd taken a long moment to study the quality of light that had fallen upon the bags now that the sun was starting to come out. She stood at the top of the step ladder, looking into the dumpster, wondering what paper or medium she'd use to paint the metallic sparks that flickered off the shiny black bags in the half light.

"Don't do it!" It was Brigid's voice, laughing.

Orion turned and saw Brigid standing a few feet away. "You'll be responsible for me then!"

"Come down. We'll negotiate later." Brigid moved forward to help Orion down. Her hand was cold and Orion hadn't remembered that it was so rough. She jumped down, keeping hold of Brigid's hand.

"It's good to see you!" Orion said in a voice she hoped wasn't too strong.

"What's in the dumpster?"

"Just those black plastic bags full of leaves. I was trying to figure out how I'd show that light that bounces off them. I was thinking maybe metallic paper, but it might have an inorganic effect, and I'm thinking those bags look like some sort of sea creatures.

"Well, that's interesting: I've looked at those bags and thought they looked like the seals out at Seal Point. You know from a distance, if the light is just right, they look black and shiny and sometimes they fall all over each other. I was thinking I'd go there and see if I might be inspired to do a big carving of them, intertwined but moving—you know, giving the feeling of movement in the stillness of wood. Intertwined, almost like snakes."

It was lunch time, and the two women walked together and got in line for roll call, talking about shapes and forms and color, their shoulders touching, their hands touching.

After roll call, Top Flite bragged to the group—not looking directly at the man who had challenged him in the morning—that he found a record-breaking ten balls that morning.

The newcomer laughed. "Yeah? Well I found sixteen."

"Oh, yeah?" said Top Flite. "Let's see."

"I got 'em in the car."

"Oh, yeah, I'll bet."

"I do. I'll show you after lunch, man."

Top Flite couldn't wait till after they'd eaten; he grabbed his sack lunch, went into the shed and then came right back out with his challenger and several other men who were apparently headed for an accounting of found golf balls in the challenger's car.

Orion and Brigid were walking toward the shed with their sack lunches as the group of men came out, and they heard one of the men say, "If he got sixteen balls, he put ten of 'em in there before he even come out this morning."

Another said, "You got that right!"

Orion laughed. "Men!"

Brigid smiled but said, "If you don't jump in and compete right along with them, you'll be left with nothing to fight for—not even somebody else's golf balls."

"You compete, don't you?"

"I compete. I joke. I do whatever I have to do to get what I want."

Brigid and Orion sat down at a bench by themselves. Brigid didn't need to collect her thoughts. She knew what she wanted. "I want to be a supervisor—the first female supervisor in San Francisco, I want to earn as much as any man in construction in this city, I want to own my own home and own my car. I want to be respected for what I do. I want my work to be respected and I want my rights and privileges as an individual human being to be honored."

Orion listened attentively, waited for more.

"As I see it, money measures the amount of respect you get. Honor comes from what you do if you do it well."

"Why is it important to you?"

"What else matters, really?"

Orion hesitated. "Food, clothing, shelter, medicine, affection, someone knowing and caring whether you're dead or alive."

Brigid was quiet for a second and then said, "I've never had to worry about those things." She looked hard at Orion. "Is that why you're married?"

Orion felt her cheeks burn, but she answered as honestly as she could. "I don't know, Brigid. I'll have to think that one over."

Brigid smiled. "Sorry. I sometimes push too hard. I'm not used to being around women in the day time."

"And at night?" Orion asked when she hadn't meant to ask.

Brigid's smile widened: "Nothing but women."

Orion felt a different burning on her cheeks. She managed an awkward smile and then bit into her sandwich. Brigid looked at her mischievously, and Orion thought she was going to say something but she didn't. Instead, she bit into her sandwich. The two women ate their lunch and returned to the topic of art.

After lunch, Brigid joined Orion and directed her to a new place on the outskirts of the golf course. They saw Top Flite on the way and said hello. They could tell by his half-hearted response and the look of desperation on his face that he was in trouble and feeling the pressure of defending his title.

"He looks pretty worried," Brigid commented.

Orion was silent for a moment and then said, "Did you ever think that maybe it's a blessing that nothing's expected of women?"

"Never," Brigid responded quickly. "Turn right up ahead after that tree, and then park."

Orion parked by a long thick row of Eucalyptus, and the two women walked through them to the bank of a creek. A small wooden bridge arched over the water and was reflected on its surface, forming a circle that was only broken by the breeze or, Orion wondered, was there a current running below the surface. The trees stood as they had no doubt stood for decades, but here, too, Orion noted the movement in the turns and bends of their trunks.

"What do you think?" Brigid asked.

"Magic. It feels magical."

Brigid laughed softly.

"Immanence," Orion said, thoughtfully. "It's a word I haven't thought of since Catholic school."

Brigid waited.

"God's presence in everything."

"Isn't that animism?"

Orion laughed. "Yes, I guess it is. Sister Mary Joan never made the comparison, though."

"You took the teachings very seriously? Got good grades and all?"

Orion laughed. "It would surprise you to know the girl I was back then. I can hardly believe it myself. But, no, I didn't get good grades. Though there was one year I got very good grades in Catechism—I had a crush on the priest who taught Religion. That was the same year they nearly kicked me out of school."

"I can't imagine you behaving badly."

"You know, it might sound silly, but it makes me sad sometimes that I can't imagine it either."

"You felt livelier then?"

"Maybe so. I don't know. Sometimes my behavior is very bad, you know, if I'm drinking. At least I think so, but I'm not sure. You know. Black outs."

"What does your husband say?"

"He doesn't, exactly. He says something like, 'Oh, you were out of control,' and I don't know what that means, really. Then he tells me to just forget it. He doesn't see that it's important for me to know."

"And what is it you're not seeing that you need to know?"

Orion stood up.

Brigid stood up next to her.

Orion started walking toward their cart. "We don't have a lot of time," she said, changing the tenor of their talk. "We've got leaves to rake and bags to fill."

Brigid smiled. "I won't force anything here. Okay."

The women were silent for a moment.

Orion spoke first. "Can we look for golf balls? Save them for Top Flite?"

Brigid nodded and took Orion's hand. She turned it palm up. Then she dug into her pockets. "I've already found three," she said, placing them gently into Orion's hand.

"I didn't know you were so soft-hearted."

"I'm not. I don't like the other guy."

Orion laughed.

Brigid said, "Top Flite's got his pride, though. We're going to have to find a way to sneak them into his bag."

"I can do it," Orion said. And then with a vigor and playfulness retrieved from she didn't know where, Orion said: "Say, Brigid, have you ever heard of manokleptia?"

"No."

"It's when people sneak into department stores and leave things on the counter."

Brigid laughed her too loud laugh, and Orion was happy that the two of them seemed to have returned to their easy way of being together.

When the cart had been filled for the last time before end-of-day roll call, and Orion and Brigid had found eight golf balls between them, they drove the long way back, going around to the pond that, Brigid told her, was fed by their creek. The sun was high and strong, but the wind had picked up and was softly shaking the rushes that lined the shore. The water sparkled, and again Orion considered ways of capturing reflected light, a smooth hard white surface, the brightness coming from the surface itself, not from metallic paint. Not from acrylics. Everything else darkened, the paper itself free to sparkle in thin lines that, if she were clever, would look etched, released brightness. Her eyes which had been scanning the surface of the pond, stopped. She thought she saw someone standing waist deep in the water.

"Brigid. Do you see someone out there?"

"Where?"

"Out there." Orion pointed.

"Why, yes, and if I'm not mistaken, that's Top Flite." Brigid stood up on the seat of the cart. "Hey! Hey, Top Flite! What are you doing out there?"

The man looked up, but didn't see them at first.

"Over here. Top Flite!"

He saw them, then, but was confused. "Who's that?"

"Brigid. It's Brigid. Come on out of there!"

Top Flite started to walk toward them and, as he did, the women could see he had a small net bag with him with a few golf balls in it.

"There's a lot of balls in that pond there."

"Not too many brains, though, huh?"

Top-Flite tried to smile. "I got 20 balls now, some of 'em is new ones, too. I can probably sell 'em."

"Those aren't 20 balls," Orion said, suddenly familiar, bolder than Brigid had seen her before. "Not more than five in that bag."

"No. I got 'em back at the shed, locked up in the supply room. No one can get to 'em." Then drawing a key out of his shirt pocket, he said, "See."

Brigid saw a sudden smart bright look cross Orion's face. "Drive will you, Brigid," she said, and then she turned to Top-Flite. "Come on," she said, a freshness in her manner. "We'll be late for roll call. And you'd better take your shirt off and let the sun dry it a little before we get there. If she sees you like that she might want to test you with a Breathalyzer. You can use my jacket."

"You think so, Brigid?"

Now the women exchanged a quick glance. "I wouldn't be surprised.'

As they started back, Top Flite removed his shirt.

"Hand it to me. I'll put it on the windshield."

Top-Flite did as he was told, suddenly shivering.

"Say, you ladies wouldn't happen to have a little drink on you, would you?"

Brigid said: "No, but we're near enough to the snack bar. We'll drop you off, take these bags to the dumpster, and be back for you in a few minutes."

"That's mighty nice of you, ladies."

"That's the truth," Orion said as the two women drove off.

*   *   *   *   *

"Want to go out for dinner? Some of the guys are going to watch the game at Ed's Place. You know, pizza and beer. Regular great cuisine." Orion smiled. "They have salads, too, if you want."

"Sure. Maybe I'll just stay for a while. I've got something I want to sketch tonight. It's a..."

"Okay. That way, if it turns out they want to play a few hands of poker after, I wont have to say no."

"Are there times you say no?"

"How were the convicts today?"

"Really good. There was a contest, and..."

"Good. Well, the game starts in an hour. We'd better change. I'll make you a drink. Bring it into the shower."

"I'll take the drink, but if we only have an hour..."

Frank winked. "We'll have enough time."

CHAPTER NINE

Complications

It was a long week, and Saturday morning roll call was a disappointment. Brigid gave Orion a vague smile. Then she disappeared, off in a Cushman. Orion had her own cart, and she took off too, but in a different direction, ending up at the creek.

The fog was thick there near the water, but Orion could see the dark side of the Eucalyptus leaves turn in the morning breeze and flash their silvery side. It looked playful to her. Behind the trees stood a thick bank of white fog. It could have been a waterfall, and it reminded Orion of something. It was the Saturday matinees at the Sunset Movie Theater. She used to go there to see Bat Woman. Bat Woman had a cave behind a waterfall. Orion looked dreamily into the misty wall, imagining Bat Woman emerging, her black boots supple and snug like the closed wings of a bat, her mask the open wings, and in her right hand a whip, ready to draw blood.

"My hero," Orion said aloud. To herself she allowed the questions she wouldn't dare articulate. They had something to do with home being a hideout, and with her not being heroic, not at all.

Orion looked upstream to the bridge. There the mist rose like smoke from the water. The blackness under the bridge, the still discernible circle made by the reflection of the bridge and the bridge itself, forming a dark tunnel, a place she could enter alone and lose herself.

"Do I find you ready to jump again?" A voice from across the creek.

"Brigid?"

"Over here."

Orion saw her then, a few feet from the bridge. "I didn't know you were here."

"Yes, well, I figured that." Brigid started moving toward the bridge. "Deep thoughts?"

Orion just smiled and went to meet her.

As Orion approached her, Brigid said, "I come here a lot, mornings usually. I guess this will be my last one—officially anyway. I guess there's nothing to stop me showing up here now and then on weekends, though."

The women were now elbow to elbow, leaning against the rail, overlooking the creek. "That would be nice," Orion said. "I'd like to see you." Orion felt the question in Brigid's look. "I wondered where you slipped off to after morning roll call."

Brigid smiled. "Oh, you did?"

"Yes," Orion heard herself say.

Brigid was silent for a moment. Then she straightened her back and turned Orion toward her. "You know I'm a lesbian?"

Orion nodded and said, "I think I knew right away."

"Well, I may be out of line here, but I'll make my policy statement just in case: I don't see married women or bi-sexual women or women who wished they weren't lesbians. I don't bring complications into my life. This is my policy. Political and personal policy. Anything else is nothing but heartache. And it's wrong for me."

"Brigid, something important is happening to me. I think it's because of you."

"I don't want to be the one to make it happen," Brigid said with too much force. Then she smiled and shook her head. "But I certainly don't want it to be anyone else."

Then she said, "It may not even be what you think. Sometimes straight women get around lesbians and they see the freedom, feel the energy, and they connect it with sexuality. Well, maybe it is connected, but I've met straight women who have the same charge to them. It may be something else going on with you."

"Of course I don't know."

"Do you ever spend time with women? I mean straight women?"

"Usually I'm with my husband's friends. Their wives. Now and then I do something with someone at school, but there aren't many single women who want to hang out with married women, you know. They're usually looking for guys."

"Have you ever had an affair?"

"No." Orion's eyes were suddenly filled with tears. That surprised her, and what she said surprised her, too: "Sometimes I feel like I'm dying."

Brigid patted Orion on her shoulder and then took her

hand. "Let's go wash our faces in the creek."

Orion smiled. "Sounds good."

There was a bit of sun now filtering through the fog and the leafy dome over the creek. The two women found a small patch of it along the creek and there washed their faces and their hands, drying them on their jackets. As they stood to leave, Orion took Brigid's hands into hers. "Thank you," she said, and then she gave Brigid a sweet kiss that they both kept innocent. They left the place, heading off separately, going back to work, letting things settle.

At lunch in the shed Captain Cushman, orange soda in hand, made a toast to Top Flite, "the undefeated champion of the Golf Ball Retrieving Open Tournament here at Pacific Pines where finding your balls is not easy."

Top-Flite was delighted. He stood up on a bench to receive the applause that now came from the forty or so inmates gathered in to eat their lunches. A few of the men and one woman added their testimonials. The younger man who had challenged Top Flite even managed, "Yeah, well, I don't know how he did it, but he did it." Then, with his lip curling as he tried to smile, he mumbled, "Congratulations."

Brigid was delighted. Orion was too, and they talked about the competition and about their work plans for the afternoon, and about anything at all except what was on their minds. It was not until afternoon roll call was taken that the two women turned to say goodbye.

Brigid walked Orion to her car. "I'm giving you my phone number. It's not listed. I'd like to hear how you're doing, and I'd like to see you, too, but... I'm going to ask you something."

"What?"

"Do you think you could go a month without a drink?"

Orion was aware of a sudden loss of breath.

"Why?"

"Because I don't think I'm going to be strong enough not to pursue you and you're married and you don't know what's happening to you. This could be the beginning of a terrible upheaval for you, and if I'm anywhere around it, it'll affect me, too. You're going to need every bit of clarity you can muster. And I want to know something about how serious your drinking is."

Orion smiled. "A month of no booze and you'll see me?"

"Orion, I've had experiences with women who drink. And I had one affair with a married woman. But I have never had the bad sense to see a married woman with a drinking problem. It would be hard for me not to see you, but I won't let myself in for that much trouble."

Orion looked at Brigid for a long time, wondering if this woman or any woman or any human being was worth a month without a drink, wondering if she could actually do it, thinking that either way she'd lose.

Brigid broke into her thoughts. "You know, Orion, putting us aside, it really shouldn't be such a hard thing to go a month without a drink."

"I don't think it is," Orion countered, though she felt as though it was and she would lose…what, she didn't know, but she was frightened.

"This is hard on you. I'm sorry. But could you just try? Just to see how things are?"

"You think for sure I'm an alcoholic?"

"I don't know. Blackouts are a sign, I'm told."

"I'll call you in a month. It's not going to be a problem for me, really."

"I hope you're right for your own sake."

Brigid took Orion's hands into hers and kissed them. Orion felt the kiss move up her arms and into her chest. My god, she said to herself. My god.

As Orion drove up 24th Street on her way home, she noticed the florist shop, and she slowed down. Was she forgetting someone's birthday? Was someone sick? She drove around the block, trying to think of what it could be. When she passed the shop the second time, she saw some yellow flowers. Those were pretty. She had an urge to buy them for herself and put them in her studio or…she could lie down on some grass somewhere and have yellow flowers in her hair and on her breasts. She had never bought flowers for herself before. She stopped the car. She sat for a minute. Then she started the car back up and drove off.

CHAPTER TEN

The Drink
She Didn't Have

Orion hadn't had a drink—not even wine with dinner. She noticed that Frank didn't notice. Did she expect him to notice the absence of something? Absence to absence, she thought. Dust. Hope. Resurrection?

Orion went down to her studio. She had a mirror that she used to look at her work from different perspectives. This time, she placed the mirror in front of herself and looked at her face. She studied her eyes. How could such tiny disks contain so much information? Microchips. But they apprehend beauty, as well. There was beauty in her eyes, she saw. Flecks of yellow and green lighting her light brown eyes. Her hair, which she had always hated, tonight seemed different. She saw beauty there, too, in the tones of red and the dark brown and some light reflecting strands of blonde—or maybe that was gray. Either way, it looked pretty to her. It had always been wild, disobedient hair. She tousled it so that it looked even wilder, like thick flames. Like the flame-fish of Matisse.

She lifted the curls that covered her ears, and she smiled. They were comical, ears. They seemed to have been stuck on as an afterthought, like left over dough for a piecrust. Fungus on trees sometimes take that shape. It's funny you can close your eyes, but your ears are always open. They could have been made to open and close, though. That little flap there closest to the cheek, just above the lobe, it could easily have been made to open and close like an eyelid. It would be an earlid. Though why would she ever want to close her ears? Really, hadn't she been waiting all her life to hear the right questions? What were they? Well, she didn't know, but she did know it was questions and not answers she wanted to hear. Answers were so rarely satisfying. They make you wish upon a planet. She was in a silly mood, but what a thing it is to be a creature with all these silly parts and ridiculous openings and yet to have so many longings and aspirations.

Orion wanted, suddenly, to hear beauty. She ran upstairs to the music shelves and found "Lakme," then switched the studio speakers on, set the player to repeat, and ran back down the stairs.

The music was there in the room. It was strange for it to be there, and it was exciting. Orion took ink and brush, placed herself again before the mirror and this time looked at the hands Brigid had kissed. She took up the brush, her hand moving reverently across the porous white paper that received the ink. She made quick drawings with bold strokes, and she made dozens of them, all of her hands. When the music had played through several times, she went back upstairs and played just "The Flower Duet" through once, and again, and on the third listening, she finally heard what she'd been listening for—not the words, she didn't know the meaning of the words. In fact she couldn't have found words to describe what she was hearing in her heart, what was filling her heart and overflowing, what finally released the tears that had been building all night, though she had not felt sad. Orion allowed the tears to fall, trusted what was happening in her heart, and did not have a drink.

When the tears stopped, Orion stretched out on the carpet and let the music play out, nothing happened at all in her head except the music, and when the music was over, she rose, feeling new energy in her bones and muscles and vibrancy upon her skin.

She felt fluid and strong and open. She found Debussy. She danced. In her room. His sea music moving her across the carpet. But when that music ended she found herself slightly melancholy, and she thought of the drink she wasn't having.

Then she remembered: there had been a brochure about a workshop somewhere. She went through several desk drawers before she found what she was looking for. The brochure was pink and purple and lavender and red, colors ordinarily unlikely for Orion, but tonight they were exactly the right colors, exactly.

It was a two-week workshop in Santa Cruz for women artists starting in three weeks. School would be over then and she would have served her time at Pacific Pines. In fact, her last roll call would be about two hours before the first session started in Santa Cruz. Orion realized she'd be away from San Francisco when her month was up, when it was time to call Brigid. Well, she'd call her from Santa Cruz. Maybe that would be better, anyway. She'd be away from Frank and school and maybe, in the Santa Cruz hills, working all the time on what she loved, things would fall into place for her; she would know what to do. She would not drink. Because of her promise and because she knew she had to be as clear as possible, she would not drink for the next twenty-nine days. She could manage it.

It was almost one in the morning when Orion filled out the application. There was nothing in it about design or composition or materials. She wondered exactly what it was they were offering. "Well, I'll call them Monday and see," she said, but then she decided, no, she wouldn't call. She'd just go and find out. She needed to work on control, controlling the brush more. It seemed to have gotten away from her lately, the lines growing larger and thicker when she hadn't meant it and then wetter, thinner, when she hadn't meant it. Well, part of it was that she was running out of patience. She noticed, from the uneven tones, that she was not loading the brush properly, not fully pushing the ink to the center bristles, not fully soaking or stroking the brush. She was losing patience with the brush, losing control. But then she looked again at the sketches she'd made of her hands, and she saw that she liked them. They were very different from what she'd done before. These hands, these renderings, were very forceful, even when they were posed at rest. It was the life in them showing. They were good.

She returned to the application, signing it with her new name. Orion Devon. There was a neat repetition in the shapes of her first name and her last. The endings closed so that they fell like cliffs. She said her name out loud. Orion Devon. The sound of the endings—the nnnnnnn—broke the fall. Then it brought to her the sound and image of bees scouring a field. Remembering Brigid's kiss, she brought her hands to her own lips and kissed them. It felt friendly when she did it. She wondered how it had felt to Brigid.

Orion sealed the envelope, put a stamp on it, and went out, walked down the hill into Noe Valley, and found a mailbox. When she pulled back the painted metal door and placed the envelop upon it, she had an odd notion that her life was about to change. She hesitated for a moment and then, of a sudden, she released the handle. The banging of the door startled her, and as it shuttered to stillness, she felt a shiver rush through her body.

When she got back home, she did not have a drink. She went back down to her studio and packed some special things for the workshop: her Kolinsky red sable brushes, the flat hake brushes for washes, and the pure squirrel mop that was hand-cupped with brass wires. She packed her best slate stone and five new ink sticks, all black. It was after two o'clock when she went to bed.

At five o'clock the alarm went off; yet with only a nap, really, Orion felt fine. At Pacific Pines, she missed Brigid as she raked and bagged leaves, but she had to admit she felt hopeful about herself. She had a feeling that things were possible. She had a sense of possibility.

When she got home, she told Frank about Santa Cruz, and he was all for it, in spite of the expense. In fact, they laughed together remembering the last time Orion had dragged him down there to the University of California for an art exhibit. They'd gone to a one-man showing of a modern artist who did portraits, interpretive portraits. At some point, Orion asked Frank if he liked any of the portraits.

"Yeah," he said. "They're all going to be just fine once they're finished." He could be witty. He was bright. His whole life had been scholarships and trophies and getting ahead on a highway that seemed nearly without obstacle, going from one promotion to the next, headhunters finding him to offer him more and more and more. There had, it seemed, never been a question of survival. It was for him only a question of how much success he would have how soon. His first marriage had failed, though, and he never spoke of it, except to sometimes laugh about it. His children did mean something to him, but, again, they were no trouble. They were little Franks, getting scholarships and winning trophies. None of them, she realized, would enjoy questions that don't have answers. There would be no payoffs, no percentage. Ah, she didn't know. Wouldn't she be far better off if she had some idea about payoffs and percentages. She had made a deal, hadn't she, by marrying Frank. There would be no questions asked. Neither would there be mystery. There would be silence.

*   *   *   *   *

This time as Orion drove the winding road up to the campus, the brown hills of Santa Cruz undulated like ocean swells, like the curves of a woman's body. The sun was low in the sky, and as she reached the redwoods, the trees were glowing with color. Cadmium red…no, cadmium yellow and golden ochre, maybe very thinned out cerulean blue or ultramarine for the deeply chiseled lines that ran the length of the tree, cutting through the bark like a million tiny bolts of black lightning. Not black, not blue-black or blue…burnt umber. Orion could build layers of yellow and gold and red and umber, a thick impasto, and then scratch rough vertical lines into it for texture. Texture and color. These colors. These colors. A flash of heat ran across her cheeks.

She rolled down the window, felt the crisp ocean air, breathed in the mixed aroma of the trees, redwood and cedar and oak and eucalyptus, and there was wild sage, too. But the slanting light. The redwoods. These colors that day. The crimson light on the Lake. The girl that night.

*   *   *   *   *

Dierdra rolled over on top of Carol and pinned her hands back over her head. Carol was as strong as Dierdra, stronger, but she allowed it, wanting to know this thing that was happening, wanting this to be happening any way at all.

Dierdra stayed arched over Carol, bending to kiss her, pushing away to whisper again that she loved her. Then she stroked Carol's face, tracing her nose down to her mouth and then pressing her finger into a corner of Carol's mouth. Carol kissed her finger. Then she opened her eyes and looked at Dierdra.

"You've done this before?"

"I have, sort of, but it wasn't like this. Not like this, Carol, I swear. This is different. Today, all day, I thought of you and my body was like an animal's body and I wanted to spring on you."

Carol smiled, "That's practically what you did."

Dierdra laughed. "I know."

"Do you know what I want to do?"

"What?"

"I want to kiss you…down there."

"Yeah, I know. I mean, I knew that night you said you were

looking at my socks." The girls smiled. "I knew, but I wasn't absolutely positive that you would really do it if I let you know I wanted you to. You know what I mean?"

Carol nodded.

"But I just couldn't stand it. I had to know. I couldn't leave without knowing. And today, I don't know. I couldn't think of anything else. I'm in love with you."

"Can I kiss you...there?"

Dierdra responded by rolling over and jumping out of bed. "I'll be right back. Don't worry. It's the first day of my period. It's light, but I want to wash. You've never tasted me before, and I want to be sweet for you. I don't want to scare you. Are you scared?"

"No. Yes. I don't know, but I know I want to." Dierdra started to leave. "Wait. I'll go with you. I can't wait here. We can take a shower together."

The girls grabbed their towels and ran down to the shower room and then into the stall farthest from the door. They undressed quickly and embraced, their young hearts thumping wildly against each other, the girls feeling their bare skin, their nakedness together, the girls wild to know each other.

"Wait," Dierdra said, and pushed away. She turned the water on, too strong and dead cold, and they both jumped back and nearly screamed. Dierdra adjusted the temperature, let the water fall over her and then made room for Carol. Carol looked and didn't look at Dierdra's body, the flesh, the curves, the shock of red hair and the spray of freckles, like powdered cinnamon, on her shoulders. Carol stepped in, took Dierdra by the shoulders, gently, took one nipple into her mouth. She heard Dierdra's moan. Then her hands pressed harder into Dierdra's shoulders and she thought she might swallow the nipple, the breast, the whole body.

"Carol, you're hurting me."

"I'm sorry."

"It was just a little. Come here." Dierdra pulled Carol's face close to hers. She put her tongue gently into the corners of Carol's mouth. "I love the way it goes in just there." Then she kissed her very sweetly, pulled back for a moment, reached for the soap and handed it to Carol. "Soap my back?" she asked, turning so that Carol had those freckles right in front of her.

"I need to taste something first," Carol said as she bent her mouth to Dierdra's shoulders and licked and kissed the cinnamon freckles. Then she took the soap into her two hands, built a lather and began to massage the golden flesh that shimmered there, that glowed there, with her hands on it. She moved her hands around to Dierdra's breasts. Dierdra stepped back into Carol's embrace so that she could reach and touch her everywhere, and Carol bit, gently, into the nape of Dierdra's neck, and, gently, circled her nipples with her two hands, just as she had circled her own so many times in this very shower. Her hands knew absolutely what to do. She was no longer caressing, but fingering, and she couldn't be sure that it would feel the same way to Dierdra as it did when she had touched herself the same way, but it was all she knew.

Again she heard Dierdra moan, and then she felt Dierdra's legs began to shake. Dierdra whispered, "Let's go back to the room." She turned and embraced Carol, her nipples hard, her tongue seeking those corners of Carol's mouth, and her hands, finally her hands, on Carol, pressing her close from behind and rubbing her in front, so that she was held and played like a harp or a bass or some sort of fire drum that might burst into flames.

Carol could feel herself throbbing against Dierdra's fingers and then, suddenly, Dierdra entered her, and Carol's legs went weak. Dierdra said, "You want to kiss me there, don't you?" And Carol could only nod dumbly in her hands. "I want you to. I want you to put your tongue way up there," she said, and she showed her where and Carol thought she might faint. Slowly Dierdra withdrew her hand and released Carol.

The girls held each other, both trembling. Dierdra rinsed off whatever soap might still be on them, and then she turned off the water and handed Carol a towel. The girls wrapped themselves in their towels, grabbed their clothing, and went back to their room.

Dierdra lay back on her bed and watched Carol towel off the water in her hair. "You have beautiful breasts. Brown nipples. Big brown nipples. Let me have one in my mouth."

Carol had suddenly frozen and could hardly step toward Dierdra's bed, and when she did she felt as if she were moving along under water, at the bottom of the sea. And she felt her balance go, some surge in the tide had pushed her, and she nearly fell into Dierdra's arms.

"Come here," Dierdra whispered, and she took Carol's breast fully into her mouth, so that now Carol felt herself pulled out of herself and into the sea where she might dissolve, and she heard herself saying, "Ah," and "Oh," and then "Ah" and then feeling the ocean inside herself reaching for the current of her breast.

Then Dierdra's hands were again holding her, playing her, pulling her further into the current. Surge and surge and surge, no longer dissolving, but gathering, as infinitesimally small organisms gather in midnight seas, gather and rise, gather and rise and grow bright rushing together, gathering, rising, rushing, growing bright and, finally, they burst out onto the surface of the sea in one enormous unstoppable body of light.

Carol started to scream, but Dierdra covered Carol's mouth with her own until the scream dissolved back into the body of light that lingered and lapped at her own spent body, Dierdra's hands still sweetly upon her, soothing her.

Tears ran down Carol's cheeks, and Dierdra kissed them and said, "I love you with all my heart," and Carol felt something opening in her chest, and she said, "This is love, isn't it?" and the girls held each other filled with each other and with the wonder of themselves in love.

Later Carol asked, "Have I lost my virginity?"

"I don't know. I think you're supposed to bleed or something. Not your period but some other blood from some small covering. It's called a hyphen or something…inside, up further, maybe. I don't know."

"Is it like this with a boy?"

"I don't know."

"You mean you've only done this with girls?"

"Girl. One girl. At school. Last year. We did it a lot, but I swear it never got to be anything like this. Are you jealous?"

"No. I'm never jealous."

"I am."

"What for?"

"I can't help it. I get really jealous."

"Well, you are the very first one, you know."

"I know. That makes me happy. I only wish you hadn't been so distant after the park. You know we've waited till practically the very last minute."

"What do you mean? Is the roof done?"

"Just about. When I called my dad I really was going to go home, but then he told me that I was coming home for sure on Tuesday or Wednesday, so I told him that he shouldn't pick me up tomorrow morning—I lied and said I wanted to stay and help you study for some big tests on Monday. He said, 'That's very kind of you, Dierdra.'"

Dierdra smiled and so did Carol, but Carol didn't feel quite right about the way Dierdra was imitating her father, sort of making fun of his good nature or something, and she also didn't understand how Dierdra could be going on in such a lighthearted way when she'd just told Carol that she'd be leaving forever on Tuesday or Wednesday. Not to lose a moment herself, not to waste it on questions and worry, Carol shrugged off her misgivings, and tried to concentrate on what Dierdra was saying.

"Anyway," Dierdra continued, "he said that they'd talked to the Mother Superior and that the roof was just about finished. All they had to do was paint some trim or something." Suddenly Dierdra sensed something was wrong. "We will still see each other, Carol, won't we?"

Carol was afraid to talk. She took Dierdra in her arms, and felt something new in her heart...no, something she had felt all her life, and it was here on this girl's neck, on this girl's breasts. She had no words for it.

"I'll kiss you now where I've been dying to kiss you," Carol whispered. Then, confused by her own passion, Carol surprised herself by standing up and trying, instinctively, to make all of this less serious, playful.

"Pretend you're putting your socks on," Carol said. Dierdra smiled and did as she was told, her right foot on the floor, her

left on the bed. "There. Just like that. Stay like that." Carol
got down on her knees and pulled Dierdra closer to the edge
of the bed. "Let me fix your sock for you," she said, and kissed
Dierdra's ankle. Then she spread Dierdra's legs further apart and
kissed her inner thighs and licked her inner thighs and she put
one finger just a little way into Dierdra and she felt the wetness
and she continued to kiss her thighs and her legs and to feel the
wetness and to spread that wetness over and in and around the
folds and chamber that Dierdra was letting her enter.

Carol withdrew her finger, pressed down on Dierdra's legs
with her two hands, and flicked her tongue across the spot her
finger just touched. "This is where you want my tongue?" Dierdra pulled in her breath as a yes. Carol flicked her tongue across
Dierdra once more and then she plunged it down into her. She
heard Dierdra murmuring, "Oh, god, Carol. Oh, god, Carol,"
and Carol felt nearly a god or some sort of deity, superhuman,
powerful to be so full of passion herself and to make this girl
cry out. "My god," was in her throat as she entered and withdrew, kissed and licked and entered and withdrew, as she loved
Dierdra with every bit of life in her. Then, remembering that
she'd hurt Dierdra in the shower, and realizing how strong her
own passion had become, she deliberately loosened her grip and
moved more gently. She sensed, through the give in Dierdra's
body, that she'd done the right thing.

Now Carol could concentrate on what she was experiencing.
She tasted strawberries and garlic in her mouth, and she wanted
to eat them whole. But she went gently, quickly and gently,
and then she felt the surge begin its move through Dierdra,
and she wanted to scream for joy herself, but she held herself
there, quick and gentle, steady, steady, and she felt Dierdra's legs

begin to shake. Dierdra pulled her legs together, closing around Carol's ears, cradling her there at the center of everything. They were part of this great thing. There was nothing else.

CHAPTER ELEVEN

Betrayed

After Orion had picked up her room assignment and taken her things in, she joined the rest of the women at an after-dinner reception in the faculty dining room. Orion hadn't had time to cook or even to stop on the way down to Santa Cruz, so she was grateful for the fruit and cheese and bread. She stopped at the dessert table—odd because she rarely ate sweet things—and stood there for a long time, looking at the curling dark chocolate that topped the cheesecake, and the cheesecake itself which looked very creamy and soothing. There were éclairs, too, and brownies and lemon pie. All the desserts were on delicate white china dishes. The tablecloth was white, too, so that all the color came from the desserts. Even the cheesecake was rich and yellow against the pale whites.

"Looks good, doesn't it?"

Orion noted a slight Jamaican accent in the question.

"Yeah, it does."

The woman reached a muscular brown arm passed Orion and picked up a cream puff and an éclair.

"I know one of these things isn't going to be enough. What are you going to have?" she asked, ready to hand something to Orion.

"I don't think I will, but thank you."

The woman smiled and shook her head. "You've got more will power than I have. I guess that's why you're so little and I'm so big." Orion saw that the woman was big. She was shapely, though, strong looking.

"Are you a sculptor?"

"No," the woman smiled. I just work out a lot. I love feeling strong, even if I'm not strong enough to say no to dessert. Say, what's your name?"

"Orion Devon."

"Oh, you're on the list to room with us. My name's Calla. Come over and meet your household," she said, indicating a group of women at a nearby table.

Calla introduced one of the women at the table as her partner, and Orion wasn't sure if that meant in business or in life. Her name was Mary, and she was a sculptor.

The other women were new to each other and introduced themselves to Orion. There was one more sculptor in the group, a small woman, who worked with neon. The other three worked mainly with oils and acrylics. Orion was the only ink and brush artist at the table, and one of the women, Rosalie, asked her if she had Asian blood. Orion surprised herself by telling the truth: "I don't know. It could be, all right."

Rosalie shocked Orion by laughing. Then she said, "I don't know what I might be either, except for my mother's white and she's not telling." Then she saw something in Orion's face, and she said, "Oh, I'm sorry. Sometimes I'm not as sensitive as I could be."

Orion smiled. "It just surprised me. Really, it's okay." But then she didn't know what to say.

Calla started talking about how she liked to work with small things, mixing pastels and oils and pieces of found art. She said people were usually surprised by how delicate her work was. "I just wonder if I appear to be graceless."

Orion rejoined the conversation. "Not at all. Probably it's just because you could sculpt and do large things. You're tall and look like you're strong."

"That's what I always tell her," the woman named Mary said, "but she has to keep asking, getting reassurance."

Orion was enjoying the openness of the conversation, the intimacy. She listened as the women talked as if they'd known each other for years, as if they'd known each other well for years, and she felt happy, and when Calla got up to get another dessert and asked if she could bring anything back, Orion said, "Yes. If there's any cheesecake left, I'd like a piece."

Calla held out her hand for Orion to slap and she did and then Orion turned her hand so that Call would slap hers and she did, and this was something Orion hadn't done or even seen since she'd left the Home. The women continued to talk and eat and laugh at the most outrageous things, and Orion felt—and smiled over the words that came to her—she felt right at home. She was at the beginning of these two weeks, she noted, and she felt the fullness of it. What came, unbidden, to her mind was an image of her hands peeling the plastic wrap from the neck of a fifth of gin, turning the screw top, lifting the open bottle to her nose, and taking in the first sharp whiff of peace—no matter what the damaging consequences might be, it always felt, at first, like peace. The whole bottle lay ahead, and even now, with nothing in her hands, she could imagine the peace. As always, right on the heels of any bit of hope she felt, any peace at all, came an open-jawed craving. She squeezed her jaws and her eyes tight, trying to erase the image from her mind, her hands rolled into fists on the table. A cold sweat broke out on her forehead.

"Hey, Orion!" Calla set the cheesecake down in front of her. "You all right?"

"Yeah, sorry. Thank you. Just thinking about something I don't need to think about." She looked down at the dessert and said, "Maybe this will help." Calla smiled. Orion took a bite and, quickly, another and another, till it was done. With each bite, the image and the craving lessened. In about one minute, she had learned that this sugar could help her craving. She would remember this for next time. She knew there'd be a next time.

There was a general meeting. Chairs were arranged in one large circle and the women, about fifty of them, were asked to seat themselves alphabetically by their first names. It was a way for them to meet each other, if they hadn't already. Then they were asked to introduce themselves to the group as a whole and to say something about why they had to come to the workshop, what they wanted from it. They were all shapes, colors, and attitudes, and apparently, none of them too good at the alphabet, as Darlene introduced herself before Betty and Marian before Lenore, and so on around the room, which gave them all an opportunity to laugh at themselves.

Many of the women were wearing shorts or jeans, some were wearing summer dresses. They were all ages, the youngest an intense Jewish girl, a freshman at Berkeley; the oldest a woman with mischievous blue eyes and long white hair that she wound in a bun that looked like spun sugar.

Most of the women were native or long-time Californians. Some had come a distance. There was one woman from Montana, a Nordic-looking housewife who was six feet tall, dressed in jeans and a cowboy shirt. When she said she broke horses, Orion imagined she could do it with her bare hands. There was a woman from Louisiana, Afro-American, probably a lesbian whose full body shook and quaked when she laughed, and she laughed a lot. Rosalie was from Hawaii, and it was hard to tell if she had a tan or if the golden cast to her brown skin was natural. She also had a wonderful smile. And there was a woman from England who was just touring through the States for the summer and happened to hear about the workshop. She was a thin young woman with thin brown hair. Her hair and skin looked dry. Orion thought that if she were to paint her, she'd do it with very dry oils, and she'd mix purple into the white of her flesh. There was something sorrowful about her.

Some of the women talked about problems with technique or materials, many expressed frustration over not having enough time to do their work, especially the married women. Some of the time, if they were married and had jobs and children, they painted at night. There was a group of them who called each other during the night and worked till two or three in the morning, and then got up at six or seven to rush through breakfast and feed the kids and get themselves off to whatever employment they had. It staggered Orion to think of it. Most of the women, it seemed, were divorced or single, and if they were working part time, the way she was, they didn't have enough money to buy materials. Orion thought of her sable brushes and Czechoslovakian paper and felt ashamed of herself, of how easy her life was and how little she produced. And she was surprised by how many women said they were hoping, here at the workshop, to go deeper into the place from where they created, and some, with no hesitation, at all, called that place Spirit, or Soul or God or Goddess. Words that were somehow not religious as they said them, but still very unexpected.

When it came her turn, Orion stumbled at first, her face hot, her jaw tight: "I haven't been around women—I mean just women—I mean without men also around—in a long time. I am surprised by the way you talk about your lives, and I'm impressed by how easily—how accurately—you seem to—I guess you do know—your feelings. And it's almost scary the way you listen to each other." Orion became embarrassed by her own honesty. "I'm very happy to be here."

"How about yourself?" someone asked.

"Well, I teach art part time at an elementary school. I'm married. I work mostly with ink and brush." Then she heard herself say, "I'd like to work more with color, with brilliant colors." The colors of the brochure flashed through her mind, and then, today, the color of the redwoods. It was true. She had been silent for a moment, but the women waited. "You know," Orion continued, "I don't always know when I'm lying," and here she paused because the women laughed, laughed like they knew just what she meant. "But I know when I've said something that is true." And she heard the women say, "Yes," or "I hear you," or "Tell it," or just murmur sounds of agreement and encouragement, and she felt as though she were being listened into speech because she kept talking. "And that's true. I need to work in brilliant colors because…I…need too… I need to shout." And she did shout by the time she got to the end, and so did some of the other women in the room; they said, "Listen to that," and "That's right," and "You're in the right place," and a few just howled or clapped their hands, and Orion was in the middle of all this.

As the next speaker patted Orion on her shoulder and said, "I need to shout too" and started talking about all the shouting she planned on doing in the next two weeks, Orion wondered about this feeling of being home, and she knew she hadn't felt it in a very long time. She also knew it was not an altogether good feeling.

She walked back to her apartment with Calla and Mary and Rosalie, and they talked for a short while and then went off to their bedrooms. Orion felt suddenly very tired. She brushed her teeth, washed her face, put on her nightgown and went to bed.

*   *   *   *   *

"Hey, Carol, are you in there?" It was Denise.

The girls both sat up as they woke up and looked at each other, not knowing if there was something they should say or do.

Carol jumped back over to her own bed, found her jeans and a shirt and put them on as she said, "Yeah, what do you want? It's early." She looked too late at the clock. It was almost ten. When had they finally fallen asleep? She looked back over to Dierdra who was almost dressed. "Wait a sec."

Carol started for the door, but stopped. The sheet they'd thrown to the floor, the towel, Dierdra's underpants—everything was a mess. Carol swooped it all up and threw the bundle into an armchair. Dierdra was attempting to get the bloody stains out of sight as Carol unlocked the door.

"What took you so long? Hey, what're you guys doing? Jeez, what a mess. I never saw your room like this before. What's going on?"

"We're just packing. I'm helping Dierdra pack."

Denise moved into the room and stood before the armchair. Then she carelessly threw the pile of things onto the floor and sat down, pulling her legs up under her, hugging them as if she didn't want to get any of this messy room on her.

"Looks like a cyclone hit this place."

Dierdra took her suitcase out from under her bed, and started taking things out of her closet. Carol joined the effort. The three girls were silent.

Finally, Denise said something. "What time are your folks picking you up?"

"Not till Monday," Dierdra answered. She stepped across the floor and over the bundle that Denise had tossed onto the floor, went back to her closet, and got some more clothes. Carol stayed on the other side of the room, folding Dierdra's things and packing them into her suitcase.

When Dierdra stepped back across the room, her arms filled with clothing, she tripped on the sheet and fell, her clothes still clutched to her breast. Denise jumped up to help. Carol pushed her away. "Look what you've done! You're so dumb!" and she started shoving Denise out of the room.

"Hey! What's the matter with you?" Denise cried, and then she saw Dierdra struggling with the bundle on the floor. "Yipe! What's that?" Denise pointed to the bloodied sheet.

"It's nothing. Her period. She started her period last night."

"Oh yeah? Well, how come she's looking so guilty?" What are you guys hiding? What were you doing in here? I knew I heard you doing something. I knew I heard you!"

"What were you doing, listening at the door?"

"What if I was? The big question is, 'What were you doing?'"

"Get out. Get out of my room!" Carol glared at Denise, but Denise wasn't moving. Her feet were planted and her face was full of triumph.

Then something happened that Carol had never seen before and would never forget. Dierdra went over to her bed table, opened the drawer, found her wallet, took out a fifty-dollar bill and handed it to Denise. "Denise," she said, "would you be good enough to leave Carol and me alone now?"

For a second Denise hesitated. Dierdra moved closer to her, and started to put the money into the pocket of her blouse. Denise stepped back and crossed her arm over her chest. In a very weak voice—one that didn't match the words—Denise said, "Don't touch me." For another second, there was no movement. Then, the arm seemed to come loose. It jerked forward like something mechanical, and it stopped, palm open, between the two girls. Carol saw Dierdra suppress a smile and then drop the bill into Denise's hand. She saw the hand close around it in one quick movement, and the fist thump back into place, like a Roman soldier's, hard upon her chest. Then without a word, Denise turned—pivoted—and marched out of the room.

Carol rushed to close the door behind Denise. Then she stood there at the door looking at Dierdra. Dierdra sat down on her bed and beckoned to Carol, but Carol found herself unwilling to join her. She was learning something, and she sensed the lesson wasn't over.

"Carol, come here. Please." Dierdra pushed the suitcase off her bed onto the floor, the clothes Carol had packed, tumbling to the floor. Then Dierdra patted the empty space next to her, the place Carol should occupy. "Come on, Carol. What's wrong?"

Carol didn't know what to say. She didn't know what it was but something was definitely wrong, and she was sure it was going to get worse.

"Carol? What is it?"

Carol heard footsteps in the hall. More than one person. She pressed one finger to her lips and scowled at Dierdra to be quiet. They heard a man's voice and then a woman's.

"Yipes," Dierdra said out loud, "it's my parents."

Immediately there was a knock at the door. "Dierdra? Dierdra, honey, are you there?"

"Dad! What a surprise. Wait a minute."

The girls rushed to throw the dirty linen somewhere—into the closet this time—and to get the suitcase back up on the bed. Carol was picking the clothes up off the floor as Dierdra opened the door, and she smelled Dierdra's mother and father before she saw them. They smelled like soap and cologne and powder, like the cosmetics counter in a department store.

"What a surprise!" Dierdra said as she threw herself into her dad's arms. Carol looked then and saw Dierdra leave her, saw the change in Dierdra's body as it both wilted and clasped, heard it in the rising tight small squeal of her voice. She entered her father's arms and, in an instant, she was gone.

"Whoa, there, young lady. I guess you really did miss us, huh?" Dierdra's dad was tall and good looking. He had red hair, too. He was wearing a dark suit and a tie with diagonal stripes. His shirt was spotlessly white.

The mother stood on the edge of the affection passing between father and daughter. She was a thin woman, very tan, her hair was straight and a shiny brown. She was wearing a suit, too, very plain and expensive looking. She said, "Well, of course she missed us," and then she patted Dierdra's shoulder. Dierdra turned and gave her mother a kiss that kissed the air, her cheek brushing against her mother's cheek, her mother also kissing the air.

Then the mother and father and daughter turned and looked at Carol. "Mom, Dad, this is Carol."

"How do you do, young lady?" "It's so nice to meet you. Dierdra's told us a lot about you."

Carol smiled as best she could. "Hello. Thank you. She has?"

"So," said the father, "this is where you've been all this time. A little cramped, isn't it?"

"Oh no. It's been fine. Anyway, not much longer. What brought you over here this morning?" Dierdra asked.

"Well, darling, I thought maybe you could use another bag. You know you've taken a lot more over here than you've brought back home." The mother looked carefully around the room as she talked.

"We were on our way downtown, anyway, so it was no trouble to stop by. I don't need an excuse to see my baby, do I?"

Again, Dierdra found her father's arms. "Of course not, daddy."

"I see you've already started packing," the mother said, moving toward the open suitcase.

"Yeah, and you're right. I don't have nearly enough room."

The mother stopped, suddenly, turned just as suddenly, and flung open the closet door. Carol looked at Dierdra, but Dierdra was frozen. "This is your closet, isn't it? My goodness, what's all that," the mother started to move forward, to take charge, explain or kill the thing on the closet floor, but a loud knock at the door stopped him.

"Dierdra? Carol? It's Sister Mary Joan. Open the door," she said, but she didn't wait. She opened the door herself and was surprised to see Dierdra's parents in the room.

Carol watched as mother and father and daughter and sister look at each other, no one looking at her, and in that instant she was the one to leave, suddenly becoming an audience.

Movement in the doorway: Denise behind Sister Mary Joan. A howl comes from Dierdra who is now pointing at Denise—not at Carol—and screaming: "She made me do it, Daddy." And daddy looking now past Sister Mary Joan at the scraggly girl his daughter was indicting, starting again to move, this time in the direction of the accused, but stopping again, confused. What was on the closet floor? Who is this girl behind the nun? Carol watched the father, interested in father moving and father speaking.

"Dierdra, I demand to know what's going on here." But then father sees fear on daughter's face. He turns. "Sister, do you know what's happened here?"

Carol looks at mother. She has stood holding the closet door open. Now she quickly closes the door and turns her back to it as if nothing at all was worth looking at in there. Carol is intrigued to see the mother's mouth form a smile, to see innocent good cheer on her face. Mother speaks: "I'm sure whatever it is we can settle it all downstairs. Why don't we go downstairs and have some tea and talk things over." Then she turned to Carol, as if Carol were still there as part of them, and said, "I think you need to straighten things up here. You can join us later."

"That's a good idea," Dierdra said, her voice still high, as she moved toward the door, mother fast behind her, and even dad ready to move away from whatever mother had moved away from, instinctively the family ready to move away from anything that might harm daughter. Sister Mary Joan already turned with only Denise unwilling to participate. Carol, herself, getting it, that she is supposed to get rid of the evidence of any wrong doing while the family drinks tea, and Carol wanting to do this for her own sake, hardly believing what was happening, but more than willing to take advantage of it.

"Oh, no you don't. You're going to blame everything on me," Denise said with a surprising amount of certainty, and she brushed past Sister Mary Joan and the family.

Carol moved and heard herself speak. "Denise, no one's blaming you for anything. Nothing's happened, has it!" Carol glared at Denise, but the girl's fear of the mother and father and Sister Mary Joan, her fear of being the scapegoat, was stronger than her fear of Carol.

"Carol, Sister saw me with the money. I told her why Dierdra gave it to me."

"What have you got to say for yourself?" Sister Mary Joan demanded of Carol. Again Carol looked at Dierdra. This time Dierdra caught her look and she said, "I didn't give Denise the money. She stole it. That's why she said whatever it is she said."

All eyes are now on Denise who is red with anger. "Liar! Liar. I'm not a stealer. Carol's the stealer. Ask her where she got the material to make those curtains and…she looked around for the bedspread. Where's the bedspread and those sheets… they're covered in blood!" she screamed as she went to open the closet door.

"Get out of here, Denise!" Carol yelled, but Denise was not going to be stopped. "They were doing something in here all night. Something queer. They're queers. And they got blood all over everything. I saw it. That's why Dierdra gave me the money. To shut me up."

Again Carol left the scene and started watching. Denise was clear—anyone could see she was telling the truth—and they would not blame Dierdra.

She watched as Dierdra ran, once again, into her father's arms, sobbing this time that it was Carol who made her do it, that she had been afraid to name Carol, but it was her, and that it was Carol that took the money from her and that it was Carol who gave it to Denise and that was why she was so glad to see daddy when he appeared at the door just in time.

Dierdra's father placed his daughter in her mother's arms and then took two quick steps towards Carol, and, although he had not raised a hand and might not have even thought of it, Carol stopped his movement toward her with her eyes.

The man hesitated. "I don't know what's going on here. Sister, my daughter has been forced into something. I don't know what. And she has had money taken from her. These girls," he pointed to Denise and Carol, "are responsible, and I want you to get to the bottom of it. First I'm taking my child home. I'll come back for her things, and I'll expect a complete explanation." Then he turned to his wife, the girl still in her arms. "Let's get out of here."

Mother, father, daughter exit, their backs going out the door. Carol is left looking at Sister Mary Joan, looking at Denise. She waits. Hardly hearing the words, she sees Denise explain to Sister Mary Joan, watches as she goes to the curtains and points to Lillie's workplace, watches as Denise opens the closet door to see if maybe—yes, there they are, the bloody sheets. She sees Sister Mary Joan hold the fifty-dollar bill up in front of Denise, and sees Denise burst into tears and then turn and point at Carol.

Carol hears herself calmly confess that she forced Dierdra to have sex with her, that she was violent and caused Dierdra to bleed and that she took the money from Dierdra and gave it to Denise to stop her from telling. Sister Mary Joan easily accepts it all as the truth, nodding her head and then shaking her head as she listens. Carol sees Denise stop sobbing and listen, nearly in awe, to what Carol is saying. Carol feels disgust and laughter rising in her as she looks at the dumb expression, the disbelief on the red wet pitiful face that was now, again, filling with fear. And when Carol saw fear on Denise's face, she huffed to stop herself from slapping her. Sister Mary Joan took the sound as belligerence, and she slapped Carol hard across her face, something she had never done before. Then she covered her mouth as tears brimmed in her eyes. She made the sign of the cross. "Forgive me, Father," she whispered, eyes now lifted to heaven. Then she turned to Carol. "I'm locking you in your room. Mother Superior will have to deal with this." She took Denise by the shoulder and pushed her out of the room. Carol heard Sister Mary Joan's jangle of keys. Heard the door lock.

Carol felt that something like this had been bound to happen—really, she'd been waiting for it to happen. She'd been in the Home too long. She looked around her room, as if for the first time. Saw the work that had gone into it. The white walls still clean except for the scuff marks that Denise's dirty shoes had left on the wall by the bed. The curtains freshly washed and ironed. The bedspread gone now, tossed into the closet with the rest. The bed bare except for Dierdra's open suitcase.

Carol went over and touched the cashmere; it was not lifeless. She lifted the sweater to her face and smelled the expensive perfume—a French name—and she smelled Dierdra, her cinnamon skin. She did not kiss or bring the sweater to her cheek. She folded it neatly, returned it to its place and closed the suitcase.

On the wall before her was the Extreme Unction Crucifix she bought for herself when she first moved into the home. She'd had a fear then that she would die without being absolved of her sins. She had placed the crucifix over her bed so that, when the priest came to give her last rites, everything would be ready.

They would be sending her somewhere. Another home? Juvenile Hall more likely. She went to the closet, kicked the sheets aside and took down her suitcase. She took the Extreme Unction Crucifix down from the wall and opened it. There was a candle and holy water in it; still there was room for her cellophane-wrapped marijuana. She slid the crucified Lord back over her stash and placed the cross in her suitcase. Then she took her drawing pencils and pad from the desk and put them in her suitcase next to the cross. Her clothes, toothbrush, hairbrush. She was ready. But there was one thing she wanted to do first.

Carol let herself out through the window. As she walked past the well-tended front yards near the church, she took a long look at the small green squares of grass and at the crepe paper flowers. The sun was nearly straight overhead, bleaching the colors of everything, and there were hardly any shadows.

Carol continued to look hard at the places lining the street as she approached the Harmony House Cafe, thinking maybe she wouldn't be seeing them again. There were few nice clean stores along Temple, but mostly they were tired-looking places with greasy food and dried up old timers hanging out in them. Carol could smell the grease and the burnt coffee as she walked on down the street.

*   *   *   *   *

Monday morning the women got their group assignments from a bulletin board. Orion's group was meeting outside instead of in a studio. Just as she joined them, one of the women was introducing herself.

"I'm Rita." She looked at each of the women in the group as she talked, and made strong eye contact. "I've spent thousands of dollars on paints and on therapy to find out who and what I am." Here Rita pointed to what was written on her T-Shirt. It said "Tex Mex Dyke."

"One day, in El Paso," Rita continued, "a kid shows up at my door. He tells me he's an artist and he knows I'm an artist, too. He had his own T-shirt printing business in his house just down the street from me. I don't know if he already had some made up or if he made them especially for me, but this is just red dye and black stencil ink. It probably cost him $2.00 and ten minutes to do it. Anyway, this was the suburbs, and I was married to white man, you know, eating sour cream on my enchiladas, minding my own business, when this boy shows up and tells me what I didn't know I knew until he told me. He handed me this T-shirt and when I read it, I just laughed out loud. I told that boy he had cajones all right. Later we got to be good friends. Now I order five at a time, and he puts my name on the back for no extra charge.

"Years later, when I had a girlfriend, I told her that I wished that boy had shown up a lot sooner and saved me all those years of ignorance and pain, and she said, 'If he'd come to your house any sooner, you'd have thrown him out.'"

Now Rita lit some incense that she'd placed in a clay dish in front of her. She looked up and scanned the group. Someone responded with, "When the pupil's ready, the teacher will appear."

"Eso es," Rita nodded. "I had to hear it the way I heard it when I heard it." Now her already intense eye contact deepened, and it seemed to Orion, stayed too long on her. "Today I am your teacher," Rita said. "What will I need to say or do to help you get where you want to go with your work? I don't know yet. I have some ideas, of course. But the first thing I need is something from you: radical trust." Orion didn't like the sound of it. "Okay. Let's get started. Widen the circle here for the latecomers. Your knees should be touching the knees of the women on either side of you. You'll have to sit cross legged." Orion wasn't sure she wanted to be part of this. She was trying to think of an excuse to leave.

"Are you going to join us?" Rita was talking to Orion.

"Oh, yes, sorry," Orion said as she joined the group and cursed herself for not having the courage to get the hell out of there. Jesus, she thought, I need a drink.

CHAPTER TWELVE

Comfort

The morning didn't turn out too badly. Rosalie was in the same group, and once Orion saw her, she felt less skittish. The group meditation wasn't easy for Orion, though. Rita directed them to connect the bottom of their spine with the center of the earth and then the top of their head with, of course, the heavens. Orion had the image of a spike going through the center of her spinal column. She did not feel connected. She felt spindled. All the more so as she couldn't move. Her legs went numb while every other part of her body seemed to be shot full of spasms. She did not feel empowered. She felt punished and was very relieved when the twenty minutes finally came to an end.

Their first assignment was to quickly sketch two things not ordinarily related and create a relationship through some basic form. The energy that had not been calmed but backed up by the meditation now rushed through her hands, and Orion went to work in lightning strokes. In less than a minute, she had sketched the five-pointed star in the core of an apple.

"Wow," Rosalie said, surprised. "Are you a Buddhist?"

"No," Orion laughed. "They study something forever before they draw it. I don't have that kind of patience...or depth. They really get the essence of something."

"I read that they study it for four seasons."

"Well, see, that's the trouble. No seasons to speak of. Otherwise, I'd do it."

"Don't laugh," she said, nodding at Orion's star apple, "you have got something there all right. Essence might be the word to describe it."

Orion was embarrassed by Rosalie's comments. "I don't usually show my work to anyone," she said.

"Oh, I didn't mean to...guess I'm asking too many questions again," she said but immediately left that idea for another question: "Gee, why not? You're good."

Orion didn't know what to say.

"Not too used to compliments?" Rosalie asked.

Orion surprised herself by this time answering that question truthfully: "It would be easier to get slapped."

Rosalie was quiet for a minute. Then she said, "You know what I think. I think you must be ready to change that." Then she turned to her sketch pad. "I'm very slow," she said, showing Orion her drawing, "and I'm not too sure how that shell looks inside." She was sketching a nautilus, the inside spiral repeating the spiral inside the human ear. "Secret chambers."

"Beautiful idea."

Rosalie smiled. "Compliments don't hurt me I guess—I'm always fishing for them."

It was easy being with Rosalie, so when Orion was getting ready to drive into town she asked her if she'd like to go with her. She liked her, but she also didn't want to be alone with any temptation. "I'm going down the hill to pick up a few things," she said. "We could have lunch if you like."

"Yeah. Great. I need to get some number five pencils. Could we do that?"

"Sure."

They worked a little longer on their drawings and then started down the hill. At one point they passed some students working on vegetable gardens. Separating the patches were rows of sunflowers and marigolds, with some small yellow flowers mixed in.

"Look at those flowers," Orion said. "Aren't they a gorgeous color?"

"The small ones? Yeah. The color's like sweet butter."

"What are they called?"

"I don't know. Maybe buttercups? They were in with some purple asters I bought the other day."

"What did you buy them for?"

"No special occasion. Just for me."

"Really?"

"Sure. Don't you ever buy flowers just for yourself?"

Carol laughed. "No. I'd be embarrassed...or...I don't know."

"They're not expensive, you know."

"It's not that. It's just...."

"I buy myself incense, too, anything that helps me reach that place I paint from."

Carol was quiet.

"What is it, Orion?"

"There's a flower shop on 24th Street in Noe Valley. Every time I've passed it lately, I've wanted to stop and buy some flowers, yellow ones especially…and," here she looked carefully at Rosalie, trying to gauge whether or not she could trust her, "I had a very strange urge."

"To do what?"

"To lie down and then put them on my chest, just rest them there. It was a feeling that they would give me light." She looked again at Rosalie, to see her reaction.

"Wow, you could get some beautiful images from that. Did you paint it?"

"No," Orion laughed, "I don't do that kind of thing. Anyway, it's just silliness."

"Well, sounds to me like maybe these two weeks are going to be a good time for you to do that kind of thing. Isn't that why you came?"

"Maybe. Yeah. Maybe so."

Orion parked on Front Street, half way between the art supplies and the liquor store. "The Kaleidoscope okay?" Orion indicated the restaurant across the street. "We could meet in fifteen minutes?"

"Okay. They've got great cheesecake there."

Orion was embarrassed that Rosalie had apparently watched her wolf down the cheesecake. She wasn't sitting that close to her. She reminded her of Dierdra, seeing everything and asking any kind of question. Well, she smiled to herself, maybe that's why I like her. Confusion in her heart immediately brought the need for clarity, for just a little bit of a little peace, and she knew, clearly, that even with Rosalie's company, she'd find a way to get a little something to drink. Anyway, Rosalie wouldn't have any way of knowing this particular secret, and normal people drank all the time.

"Did you forget something? Do you need some art supplies?"

"No. I've brought more than I need." She heard the irritation now in her voice. "Sorry. I was just thinking of something else. Sorry."

"That's okay. I'll just go get my pencils. See you over there in a minute." Rosalie turned and walked up the street. Orion watched her for a minute, wanting to make sure she was gone, that she wouldn't see where she was going. Not that it mattered, she said to herself, as she turned and went up the street.

Orion stood in front of the liquor store for a minute, looking at the displays in the window—the pyramids of bourbon and scotch whiskey on sale Today-Get-Them-While-They-Last—and she allowed herself to feel the deprivation of the last two weeks. She let herself feel every minute of longing. All the longing in her body. All the longing in her spirit. A terrible longing that was also sweet and dear. Her body trembled.

She pulled open the glass door leading to the air-conditioned interior full of bags of ice in windowed freezers, full of burning liquids in transparent bottles. She checked the overheard mirrors, saw she was not being watched. She could steal a couple of pints and get away with it.

Orion stood in from of the rows of vodka from Russia and England and America, all vying for the right look, the one, she smiled, that would make her feel the most civilized as she stilled or let loose the beast.

*   *   *   *   *

She slipped into the telephone booth at the liquor store near the Harmony House on Temple Street.

"Mrs. Valle? Hi. This is Carol. Fine. Thanks. How are you? All the kids okay? Yeah. Is Federico there? Thanks."

Carol studied the telephone booth as she waited. It was the color of dark milk chocolate, even the little stand where the telephone books were supposed to be but where now there was only a chain. She pulled the handle to the two-paneled door toward her, turning the light off. Then she pushed it back again, closing the door, turning the light on. She made it go off again and then on several more times. Carol looked again at the color of the walls and thought she might steal a Hershey Bar to take with her. She looked out through the octagons of green thread in the glass of the door panels. Rows of bottles filled with cheap wine and sweet whiskeys stood just a foot or so away. Carol pulled the handle toward her very quietly this time, stood just as quietly, and pressed the two door panels against the wall with her back. She looked at the overhead mirrors to see where the man was. He was opening cartons of cigarettes and stacking them onto the wall dispenser. Quickly, Carol reached out, stretched as far as she could without putting down the phone, and with an index finger and thumb took the only bottle she could reach, a pint of Southern Comfort. She pulled in to her body, glanced at the mirror again and saw that the man had not seen. She sat back down, slipped the bottle into her sling bag and quietly closed the door.

"Hey, Federico. Where were you?"

"No. That's okay. Que Paso?" She smiled as the train went

by and didn't toot.

"Hey, I'm in trouble. I think they're going to send me to juvie.

"At the liquor store across from the Harmony House.

"Escape to where?

"No. It's cool. Don't worry.

"Listen. I just called to say 'Better come visit me.'

"I don't know for sure. Crazy Denise will know.

"Well, if she doesn't, get your mom to call the nuns.

"I'll be all right. I don't think it's too bad for girls.

"Hey. Say goodbye to Sleepy Sam for me, too. Okay?

"No, don't worry. Anyway, I'm tired of the Home.

"Yeah, me too but, hey, you're coming to see me, right?

"Okay, I better go. No, I'm going back to the Home.

"Something I got to do first. Bye."

Carol left the liquor store and walked back, toward Glendale. A few doors from the Harmony House, Carol noticed a boy and girl playing hopscotch. She went over and watched them for a minute, stood against the wall, drew out her pint and sipped at it. Too sweet, but it was soothing. The hopscotch squares weren't drawn very straight, she noticed, and they weren't all the same size either, and they crossed the squares of the sidewalk.

"Jesus," Carol said to the kids, "who drew this for you?"

"Not too good, is it," the boy said, just a little bit of hurt pride in his voice.

"Would you mind if I tried?"

The boy shook his head.

"You still have the chalk?"

The boy nodded.

Carol took another sip of Southern Comfort as the boy reached in his pocket for the chalk. Carol placed the bottle back in her bag and handed it to the boy to hold for her. She went up the street a little bit, got down on all fours, and drew beautiful big hopscotch squares, working with the sidewalk squares, the 6 having the sidewalk line down its middle.

She came and got her bag. "Do you like it?"

The kids liked it and asked if they could play on it.

"It's yours," she said grandly, feeling very generous as she took another sip from her pint.

Through the red letters on the window spelling out Harmony House Cafe, Carol saw Howard sitting at the counter. From the look on his face, he was waiting for her. She was over an hour late. Carol hoped it was his plan to fire her.

She lit a cigarette and walked in smiling. "Howard," Carol's voice commanded him. She smiled to see him stand in response. "I just came here to tell you that you have been patronizing, condescending, and" needing to fill out the rhythm, "a total shit." Howard started to say something, but Carol held up her hand. "Furthermore, I quit. " She took a long drag on her cigarette and then she put it out on the clean white counter.

"You little…" she heard as she swung herself through the glass door. Yes, I am, she thought to herself, I am a little whatever-you-call me and I always will be. She felt fine now. Just fine. She looked back and saw that Howard was standing on the sidewalk shaking his fist at her. She thumbed her nose at him. He spat and continued to stand there. He wouldn't come after her, she figured, as she took another swig off her pint.

The hopscotch kids were gone, but it looked like they'd be back in a minute because their laggers were still there. Carol picked up one of the laggers—two bobby pins hooked together—went to the starting line, studied the distance to the last square, turned her back to it, and threw the lagger over her shoulder straight to 6, landing right on the number. She was pleased. She hopped to 3, stood there for a second as she made the decision to change the game, not to land one foot to 4 and the other in 5; instead she hopped on one foot to 4 and then to 5. At 5, she took a deep breath which lifted her chest as she extended her right arm, her left leg, and leaned forward, making a natural arabesque down to the lagger. She felt easy, graceful, able. Suddenly, the sweet liquor rose in her stomach, so she quickly grabbed the lagger and straightened back up. She didn't lose her balance, but now she didn't feel so easy.

Carol pushed off from 5, and turned so that she landed facing 4 and 5, still on her right leg. Another change, this time to her left foot as she followed her pattern back down to 1 and out. Carefully, she put the lagger back as she'd found it.

Another swig. Carol looked up and down the street. The old men going home for their naps, a man and a woman—business people from the looks of them, probably headed for Harmony—and a wino propped up against the liquor store wall. Telephone poles, telephone wires, pigeons, cars jammed up, waiting for the signal to change. That was what she saw. That was what she said goodbye to.

Carol wasn't so surprised to see Sister Mary Joan waiting at the door when she got back to the Home. When she saw Carol, the nun's face turned red with anger.

"Where have you been? How dare you! Mother Superior herself is out looking up and down the streets for you!" She grabbed Carol by the arm and led her through the door, down the hall and into the cafeteria, where, Carol was not surprised to see, the suitcase she'd packed was waiting. It was after lunch. No one was there. "Wait here, and do not speak to anyone." Carol looked around, questioning the necessity of the instruction. "Just be still, and don't try to escape."

Carol wanted to lie down. She was tired. "Am I under arrest?"

Sister Mary Joan glared at Carol. "No, you are not under arrest. You are not anything. You are nothing, nothing at all. A vile sinner. God's punishment is finally coming to you."

"I can take it, Sister. I think you know I can take it."

The nun drew back, suddenly remembering why Carol had been placed in the Home. She lowered her eyes, as if receiving a blow. "Yes, child," she said softly. Then, "Oh, what are we going to do with you?" Sister Mary Joan left her then, calling to someone just outside to watch the door, to guard against Carol's escape.

They would not let her out for a long time, maybe not for two years. They couldn't keep her past her sixteenth birthday. It didn't matter. Carol reached into her handbag for the Southern Comfort and took a swig. Then with a slow deliberate rhythm, she chanted, "Nothing but Comfort going South. Nothing but Comfort going South." She was moving closer now to that place she felt she had to go, though she could not see it clearly in her mind's eye and she had no name for it all. If she drew it, it would not have straight lines, no, a circle, no, a spiral, beginning before the line leading onto the pad from the upper left-hand corner. A single black line, thin as a razor's edge in the background, thick as it moved forward and thicker still as it moved toward the middle, then thinning again as it spins toward the bottom right and off. It could be a tornado, she smiled, and had another drink.

"Carol, put that away. Give it to me!"

She turned and saw Mario coming through the swinging door from the kitchen. He was at her side and had taken the bottle from her before she could protest. "Mario," she said, surprised at how feeble her voice sounded, how difficult it was to make her lips move. "What are you doing here?"

"What do you mean? I work here. Remember?" Mario slipped the bottle into his chef's coat. "Carol, you're at least half drunk. You're only going to make things worse for yourself… though I don't think they could get much worse."

"You heard?"

"Yeah. They were all in here. The girl's father, Sister Mary Joan and Mother Superior. Did you really hurt that girl?"

"No."

"Why'd you say you did?"

"Cause I know, in the end, that's all they were going to believe anyway. Just saves time."

"Yeah, well, saving time, in this case, is going to mean doing time."

Carol laughed.

"This is nothing to laugh about. Sister Mary Joan wants to send you to juvenile hall."

"I figured."

"You figured!"

Carol was surprised by Mario's anger. She tried to clear her head. "I'm sorry, Mario. I guess I'm a little drunk."

"Well, try to listen carefully."

She did. "Mother Superior is talking about sending you to

an insane asylum."

"What?"

"She thinks you might be crazy. An insane asylum."

"No!" Carol said quietly, believing it.

"Shhh."

At that moment, as Mario held his finger to his mouth, shushing Carol, at that moment, something passed through Carol's mind, and it was perfectly clear, like a string of printed words on a banner, but they weren't really seen in her mind's eye, or heard, yet she knew exactly these words: "This is not getting you what you want."

"We have to move quickly," Mario said, and he motioned for her to go through the kitchen door.

Carol hesitated for a second, sensing she was moving away from the fate ordained. Mario held the kitchen door open, and he pressed a key in her hand. "Go to my place. Up the alley." He pointed the direction. "Last rooming house on the left. Number 12. Go on. They'll figure it was me let you out if I'm not here when they get back. I'm supposed to be working now. Please, Carol, go."

"I feel like a coward."

"Fine. Feel like a coward. Only go. We'll talk later."

Carol stood for a moment longer, caught between the belief that she should be locked up and the belief that she should be free. Then she was through the door, running. When she got to the end of the alley, to the last rooming house on the left, she took the stairs two at a time up to the fourth floor. The key turned in the lock of #12. She let

herself in. The blinds were closed. She found the light switch. Then she closed the door carefully behind her.

*   *   *   *   *

"Caught you!" Rosalie was suddenly next to her, standing next to her, carrying a small bouquet of yellow roses. "I saw you through the window."

"Oh, Rosalie. Guess I was day dreaming."

"Well, here. These are for you."

Orion couldn't take the flowers, at first, and she couldn't talk either. She just stared at them.

"Yellow flowers," Rosalie said, reminding Orion.

"I know. I mean I know. Thank you," Orion said, finally taking them into her hands. "They're beautiful." Without a word, pressing back with all her strength the memory of the teddy bear Dierdra had given her, Orion walked quickly out of the store. Rosalie was right behind her.

"What happened?"

"It was the flowers."

"Wow, you've really been needing them"

Orion laughed. "How can you need flowers!"

Rosalie just smiled. Then she glanced back at the liquor store and said, "Did you want to buy something?"

"No. No, I didn't," she said. "Let's go eat." Then she added, "Thank you, Rosalie. Really, thank you."

When they got back up the hill, Orion called Brigid. Neither of them said anything about its having been only three weeks. Besides, it would be a month this coming weekend and that, they decided, was when they could see each other again. Brigid would come down to Santa Cruz.

Orion worked on her sketches all afternoon and into the early evening without a break, and when she got back to her suite she found that Rosalie and her other suite mates had cooked a spaghetti dinner. They asked Orion to join them. There was no wine. The women had soft drinks or milk, and Orion wondered if they were doing that for her benefit—if Rosalie had put it together about her standing in the liquor store.

"No wine?" she asked the table at large.

"Mary and I don't drink much, especially when we're working," Calla responded.

"Me either," Rosalie said. And that was that. For the first time in her adult life, Orion had milk with dinner. It wasn't half bad.

The women stayed and talked at the table for a long time over coffee. Orion wasn't saying much, mostly listening, but she noted again how easy it was to be with them, how easy it was to understand and be understood.

When Orion went to bed it was after midnight. The next morning, at breakfast, she would tell the women about the dream she'd had that night, and they would laugh and so would she, but when she had the dream, she had awakened in a cold sweat, terrified.

In the dream, Rita and Rosalie were molding clay figures of prehistoric man, going through each stage of human development then moving up to people like Napoleon and Marie Antoinette and then of flappers and tough guys and men with briefcases. Then, of a sudden, the figures were gone, and there was only one figure left, a man, life-size, alive, standing in front of a washbowl, shaving with a towel wrapped around him. He seemed to be looking into a mirror, but he was in profile and Orion couldn't really see it. Then, something reached through the mirror, and the man started to struggle with all his might, but the thing just took him straight through, leaving that place where the man had stood, empty. Rita and Rosalie reappeared, and Orion asked them where the man had gone. They looked up, surreptitiously, indicating God had taken him, but they didn't want Him to know they were telling her this. Orion realized then that they were working for God.

"Tell me," Orion asked, "is there really a heaven?"

And this was the last line of the dream, the line that had made all the women laugh at the breakfast table the next day but had, in the night, caused Orion to wake up terrified: Rosalie and Rita answered Orion's question proudly and in unison. "The best thing about heaven," they said, "is the new cars."

CHAPTER THIRTEEN

La Verita, Uccidera

It was late afternoon. The sun was low enough in the sky to cause Orion to shield her eyes with her hand as she looked west, down the driveway, waiting for Brigid. Ah, she thought, as she looked down at the sparkling sea, it had been a great first week. She had, seemingly without effort, begun to use colors. She started with the lines of reflected light on the black plastic bags at Pinecliff and then moved into the shapes Brigid had pointed out to her. Then, of a sudden, the shapes had opened up for her and for a while the leaves became her focus. She had used Dierdra's colors—ochre, umber, cadmium yellow, gold—and these led her to the redwoods, to the bark of the redwoods and the cerulean blue of lightning that struck the bark a thousand times.

Either the color or the movement of the lightning bolts in the trees led her to the ocean waves, the dark blue giving way to ultramarine and then to a faint delicate magenta nearly hidden in the constant motion of the sea, taking its shape from the waves. The currents below, sometimes miles below, sometimes miles wide, moving across the planet, the weight, the mass, the movement unobserved. Just these waves here that one could see. And above, the pale moon, nearly transparent in the summer sky, causing all this.

She tried to paint the stillness of the moon, a white so thin it nearly faded in the thin blue sky. She added stripes, a brighter white, crossing its face like a mask. Across the lower curve of the moon she sent the heavy dark weight of ocean waves, cobalt blue and violet. Even at the bottom of the sea some light must penetrate.

The waves, their shapes, returned to the leaves and then to a single leaf, diamond-shaped, elongated, elegant, pulling in at its dark center, luminous there. She returned to the lightning bolts and painted a single one coming down from the upper right hand side of the canvas and moving off on the lower left, continuing alone beyond the canvas.

She had attended the meditations and meetings every morning and then worked every afternoon and, a few times, after dinner, till one or two in the morning. It had been easy for her. The work. Not drinking hadn't been too hard, either. Rosalie's flowers. These women. These women made everything easy.

Orion smiled. No cooking or cleaning or ironing or picking things up and dropping them off and no banking or bill-paying or shopping or getting repairs done—that had made it easy, too. And no school work, no energy given to anyone or anything but her own work. Was this what it was like for Frank? Is this why he could succeed in the world? No energy given to anyone or anything but his own work? And his own play? He saw his children sometimes on weekends, but usually he just picked them up from Berkeley where his first wife, his first home, was. He'd take them somewhere for lunch, usually, then leave them at the house for Orion to look after till it was time to eat again. Then he'd take them out to dinner and maybe a movie. Orion didn't usually join them. She didn't fit into their lives really, and she hadn't been there the last time they came into the City. She wondered how he'd managed. Well, there were so many nice things, so many freedoms she'd felt those weekends at Pinecliff. She wouldn't mind spending a few weekends a month there. Much better for her soul than days in jail would have been... much better than days at home. Maybe it wasn't redemption she needed. Maybe it was just time to herself.

Frank was always alone, separate, even in sex—his kisses dry, empty, nothing there in his mouth, nothing coming from the heart or the gonads. Everything perfunctory, as if he learned lovemaking from a chart or a movie. But he hadn't even watched the movie kisses closely enough to know you don't just push hard dry lips at a face and call that a kiss. A tongue does not jump out at you, a ring of space around it, like a jack-in-the-box. It was supposed to be connected to the whole pull, like the wave or the center of the leaf. Not the bolt, not just striking. Where was the storm, the thunder?

She had felt something kissing other men, the few men she'd known before Frank. She tried to recall her feelings that moment with Sleepy Sam outside the Home. He knew how to hold her. He knew her. Those two things were connected.

Orion remembered the electric feeling between her and Dierdra on the boat at Echo Park. The lovemaking. She did not let herself think of the betrayal.

She looked down the drive again, and recalled Brigid's kiss, just that kiss on her hand. Orion felt her blood race. My god, she said, I want to kiss her lips.

She heard the car before she saw it. Then she saw it, and she saw Brigid wave. She waved back, she felt like jumping. Brigid drove up and stopped within a foot of her. She had to stand back to let Brigid out of the car. And then she was there, taking Orion's hands, bringing their bodies together, this time, the two touching, their arms wrapped around each other.

Orion felt Brigid's strong body against her, felt it yield, accommodate, melt into her own. The smell of her. Like trees. She felt Brigid's breath on her ear. "I have missed you."

With no hesitation, Orion kissed Brigid on the neck and then, in a voice she had not heard before, one that seemed to come from an ancient memory, spoken nearly from a previous life, she said something that astonished her and almost made her cry: "I have waited for you all my life."

Brigid held her for another long moment. Then, either unaware or not caring that they might be seen, Brigid kissed Orion on the mouth. And it was there. The whole pull. Orion felt her legs buckle, and Brigid laughed sweetly and hugged her tightly for a long time.

"Come on," she said, "help me find my room and take my things up. Then we'll go for a walk."

"You're staying?" Orion nearly screamed.

"Yeah. I wanted to surprise you."

"Oh, God, I can't believe it. You're staying! For the week?"

Brigid nodded and smiled, her straight white teeth, her sky-blue eyes, the firm, yielding feel of her, everything lit and full of something vital that Orion couldn't remember ever seeing before. She also saw that Brigid was relieved that Orion was happy she was staying. Could there have been any doubt.

Brigid said, "I called and found out there was a last minute cancellation. I'd have come sooner if I could have got off work, but I was lucky to get this week with such short notice." Brigid stopped. "Orion," she said and took her once again in her arms. "My God I've missed you!"

It was cool under the Redwoods. Leafy ferns and pine needles covered the earth. The two women started across a footbridge that crossed a soft gully. They stopped for a moment.

"Was it your last day at Pinecliff that we met at the bridge?"

"I can't remember. Maybe." Brigid smiled her straight-white-teeth smile, her eyes laughing. "I do remember my speech, though."

"Don't think of it, now, please."

"Don't think of what?" Brigid smiled again and brushed Orion's cheek with her hand. Then she took Orion's hand and placed it, playfully, on her forehead. "I vow, for this week, to have no memories, no policies, no plans." Orion waited. "This vow I make for my own sake." Then, more seriously, Brigid took Orion's hand and pressed her parted lips into the center of her palm. She heard Orion gasp. "Yeow!" she howled and laughed and Orion laughed too. "Come on," Brigid yelled. "I want you to see this place—it's just up that chunk of granite there."

They left the bridge and climbed up and over the boulder. At the top they could see the entire circumference of a quarry, most of it in the shade.

"Let's go over there to the sun," Orion suggested, and as they moved across the rim, she asked, "Is the water deep?"

"After we've warmed up in the sun a little, let's find out."

"Let's find out now!"

They reached a nest of sun-warmed boulders. They stopped, looked at each other, and began to undress, not slowly but with the awareness that they were revealing themselves to each other. And everywhere that Brigid was blonde and gold and fair, Orion was brown and bronze and dark. When they touched, though, they touched like blind people, gently tracing their hands over shoulders and arms, learning each other, understanding, being understood. They held hands for a moment. Then Brigid gave Orion a sweet brief kiss on her lips. Orion felt, once again, the pull.

"Let's jump in!" Brigid yelled, and turned away from her, facing the water.

"One, two, three!" Brigid counted, still holding Orion's hand, and the two of them jumped in. The water was nearly freezing, and when the women surfaced they screamed and howled with the cold and with the fun of screaming and howling.

"Jesus, how do we get out of here?" Orion laughed.

"Over there." Brigid pointed to the far end of the quarry where some stairs had been carved into the rock wall, and the women started to swim over to them.

Brigid treaded water for a moment. "Are you a good floater?"

"Tolerable."

"Float for me, would you."

Orion turned onto her back, arched and relaxed into the water, the slight motion of her hands anchoring her upon the water. She looked up at the sky, now the color of Brigid's eyes, and at the light filtering down through the Redwoods. She was no longer cold. She felt Brigid's approach and closed her eyes. Brigid swam between Orion's legs, spread them, placed her hands under Orion and, treading water, managed to very quickly and gently lift her, lick her, and release her.

"Come on," she whispered and they swam to the stairs. When they reached them, but were still in the water, Brigid, looked at Orion and asked, "Would you sit there on the first stair and let me look at you?"

Orion pulled herself out of the water and onto the sunlit stairs.

"Lean back," Brigid instructed in a whisper.

Orion leaned back on her elbows and as she did, she felt Brigid's hands on her legs, first her left leg which she touched and traced with just the tips of her fingers, then the right leg which she held and kissed. Then she moved back to the center. With soft lips and her tongue full and certain, Brigid tasted Orion, and Orion heard Brigid's howl in her throat and felt it rush up through her body to her own throat and she cried out. Brigid kissed her then, her lips closed, a gentle press, and she moved back.

"Don't open your eyes," Brigid said. "I just want to see you fully." Orion did not open her eyes. She didn't move at all. The wave held back, a deep heavy force poised and open, held back. "You are beautiful. Like an orchid." A rush forward in the water. "I have to taste you again." Again Orion cried out, and this time Brigid did not stop until the wave crested and broke and she heard Orion scream.

*   *   *   *   *

"So, how's the workshop?" Frank had called at the appointed

time, and Orion was in the lobby at the Reception Hall to receive it. "Wonderful. Incredible. I've never done such good work before in my life."

"Still doing the black and white scribbles?"

"No. I'm doing scribbles with color now."

"Oops. That'll mean more money?"

"Yes. Yes, it will. How are you, Frank?"

"You know how it is. Business, business, golf, business. The kids are here this weekend. Jesus they are a handful. You know, I kind of miss you."

"You do?"

"Well, I think that's just natural, don't you?"

"I guess."

"Anything the matter?"

"No. Just wondered how you're managing with the kids. Why don't you take them into my studio and let them paint?"

"All you got down there is black and white, right?"

"No. There are pastels and colored pencils."

"Nah, that stuff's too much of a mess. Think we'll go to a movie. Some action movie. Then I'll take them back."

"Well, have a good time."

"Don't you miss us?"

Orion was surprised by the question, so surprised she answered truthfully: "No," she heard herself say. "No, I'm having such an incredibly good time. My work…."

"Well, that's a hell of a note."

"I'm sorry, Frank. It's just…."

"Yeah. Your work. Wish my work was so much fun. Course it wouldn't bring home the bacon if it was, would it? Well, that's okay. I'm glad you're having a good time. You still not drinking?"

"Still not drinking. Hasn't been too hard."

"Well, of course it hasn't. Why would it be?"

"Well, I told you—"

"I'm not buying it, Carol. There's nothing wrong with you. You're just overly imaginative. That's why you're an art teacher."

"Did you ever wonder why I'm an art teacher instead of an artist?"

"Look, Carol, I didn't call you up to fight with you or get into any kind of emotional exchange here. Just wanted to say hello, how are you, how's the workshop, did you miss me. That's it. You've got to get that other stuff out of your head."

Orion was silent.

"Carol, are you there?"

"Yes. Frank, thanks for calling. I'll see you in a week. We can talk more then."

"Talk about what?"

"I don't know yet."

"What do you mean, 'yet'? You're sounding very strange, Carol. I tell you this no-drinking business is having a very bad effect on you."

"It's having a strong effect, all right. There are other things, including the work I'm doing here which is very good, Frank, better than anything I've ever done."

"Well, good work doesn't make a person weird, you know."

"It may be that I am much weirder than you know."

"Carol, I know you. You're much better off when you have a lot of real work to do. That painting stuff doesn't seem to help you at all. Now let's not talk about it anymore. When will you be home exactly?"

"A week from today, Sunday. Go ahead and play golf or

whatever. I won't be finished up here till noon or so. Then I'll stop and get something to eat on my way up the coast."

"Okay, Carol, I look forward to seeing you." Then he quickly added, "And I'll have a pitcher of martinis ready and waiting for you."

"Okay, Frank. I'll see you soon."

Orion was trembling. Why couldn't she talk to him, be understood.

They had exchanged words just before she left for Santa Cruz on Sunday. He'd come home from Pinecliff. "Time for a quickie?" he'd smiled and rolled his eyes. She was rushing to get packed, confused, too, by the events of the day, definitely not in that mood. Her attitude made him too uncomfortable for silence, made him disappointed enough to find something unpleasant to talk about.

"You know, they're starting to let those criminal work crews do clean-up in the club house at Pinecliff."

"They're probably just DWI's like me."

Frank laughed. "Carol, you've never seen these people. They are criminals, not just people who had a little too much to drink like you guys."

"How do you know?"

"Well, I didn't see much of them myself—saw a few leaving the club house today as we were going in for a beer. But some of the guys who were in there when they were told us how they'd behaved. You know, they're not supposed to go in there. One of them was really crazy, a black woman that was cleaning up the place like she was on something."

"Oh. How about the others?"

"Some kind of sexual deviant crimes probably. I hope they

aren't letting any child molesters in there. You know, I don't care what someone does in the privacy of their own home, but…."

Orion smiled to herself and then wondered if she looked sexually deviant. Did Brigid? Certainly Captain Cushman was as gentle looking as any man…well, that was probably the problem.

"I didn't tell you, Frank—guess I figured you'd never see me—but my cleanup gang has been at Pinecliff all these weekends."

"My God, why didn't you tell me? That could have been very embarrassing, Carol."

"I didn't want to put you off your game," she tried to make a joke of it, but Frank didn't find it funny at all, and he had a few more words to say about it. She didn't have to listen. She knew what he was saying. She wondered, though, what it had really all been about—this intrigue. Probably she had wanted to be visible to him. The orange vest, the people she was with, they would have caused him to see her, even in an unfavorable light. It didn't matter. She had wanted to be seen in a new light, that was all, in a light that showed her as a separate human being, a person. Maybe, she thought, he would begin to believe that she had a problem with alcohol. Now, she realized, she didn't care if he saw her or believed her or ever talked to her. She felt free as she ran up the stairs to Brigid.

*   *   *   *   *

The room was surprisingly clean, almost as though no one really lived in it. Carol threw herself upon the bed, but she was too worked up to stay there. She was ready to pop. What had she done? Why had she escaped? She was ashamed of running away. She could have taken it, whatever punishment they came up with. But here she was.

Just one big room with a kitchenette and a bathroom. Everything as clean and polished as a church. There were hardly any clothes in the closets, hardly anything in the drawers. There was a bookshelf with a lot of old books, some of them in a foreign language that looked a lot like Spanish, but she couldn't read it.

Leaning against one wall of the kitchenette was an old refrigerator. She opened it up and found there were six bottles of beer, dark beer with a foreign name on it, lying on their sides just under the ice-keeper. The beer looked expensive. She took one out anyway. Hesitated. Then pressed the rim against the aluminum trim in the kitchen counter. Holding the bottle with her left hand, she slapped her wrist hard with her right and popped the top off the bottle. She rushed it to her mouth before the overflow and took a long thirsty drink. It was like drinking cigars. She had to steady herself to stop it from coming back up. She waited a minute, then she took just a sip of the beer, held it in her mouth for a second before she swallowed it. No trouble staying down this time,

Now all she needed was a cigarette, but all that she could find—and they were in the refrigerator, too—was a tin box of little cigars, also with a foreign name on it. She lit one. It tasted like the beer. Not bad if she didn't inhale much. Carol sat at the small kitchen table with her cigar-beer and her beer-cigar, neither of which she could pronounce, and felt as though she were in a foreign country. She almost felt safe.

She got up and turned the television on, careful to keep

the sound low. The World of Disney was on. They were doing some kind of history of Disney cartoons. She watched. Saw how Donald Duck had started out looking more like a real duck and then later got his little jacket. Seemed like he got madder and madder the more human he became. Then they showed how Pinocchio went from a straight wooden puppet to looking more like a boy. They showed him change completely after he told the truth and rescued his father from the bottom of the ocean. She thought it was a dumb story. Mean and cruel, too. All the adults tricked him and kidnapped him and put him in a cage, and the Good Fairy punished him for his bad behavior. Well, maybe that wasn't dumb. Maybe that was the way it was, but anyway, she'd rather watch the duck. She wished Bat Woman were on television. She wished she had a joint.

Carol got up and turned the television off. She was about to open the refrigerator for another beer when she heard footsteps on the staircase. She stood where she was.

There was a soft knock at the door, and she heard Mario whisper, "It's me, Mario."

Carol walked over and opened the door. Mario stepped in, a brown paper bag in his arms. "Late lunch-early dinner," he said as he moved to the counter. "You smoke cigars?" he asked, indicating the ashtray. "And I see you had a beer. Don't you think you had enough today?" He paused. "Well, maybe not today."

"I was nervous."

"I guess you were."

"I'll pay you back."

"It'll be a while before you can do that. Here," he said, handing her a sandwich. "I got you a roast beef sandwich, and it's rare."

Suddenly Carol felt she might cry.

"Hey, what's the matter? It's a sandwich, not a cobra."

Carol smiled. "I like cobra sandwiches. Didn't they have any cobra sandwiches?"

"Fresh out," he said as he covered the table with a tablecloth and then put down two glass dinner plates. He put the sandwiches on the plates and then spooned out some coleslaw. He got himself a beer. "I brought you some iced tea with lemon. It's nice with roast beef." He transferred the tea from the paper cup to a tall heavy glass that matched the plates. "You'll like this," he said, as if they were very old friends or family. Suddenly Carol felt apprehensive, afraid to pick up the sandwich, to take a drink. How would she pay for this?

"Don't worry, Carol," Mario said, reading her thoughts. "I got another place. I just keep this place from when I owned Harmony so's I wouldn't have to go clear across to Silverlake—where I live—just to take a nap or read in some peace and quiet."

Carol was embarrassed and quickly changed the subject. "What happened after they found out I was gone?"

"Well, if it was anyone else they'd have thought it was a miracle you got away, but everyone knows you're a regular Houdini, so they didn't seem to be that surprised. They have a big search party going. The priests, the nuns, the police—The Authorities—are looking for you."

"What'll they do if they catch me?"

"They won't. It's just a show. Anyone in this city doesn't want to be found isn't found. Anyway, I got a plan. Don't worry. We'll get you someplace safe."

Carol could feel tears again. She took another big bite out of her sandwich and drank half the tea.

"What! That'll give your tummy too much to do too fast," Mario said, tapping Carol's arm. Somehow, the touch helped stay the tears.

"Guess I was thirsty."

"Yeah, it's a funny thing: alcohol makes you thirsty. Don't have anymore, okay?"

"Okay."

"But, otherwise, make yourself at home. Anything that's here, you can use or borrow or whatever. Try to get a good night's sleep. Read yourself to sleep. You ever do that?" Carol shook her head, "Well, I think there's a documentary on to-night, something about tigers, the jungle."

"Just animals eating other animals, I'll bet."

Mario laughed. "Too strong a dose of reality, eh?"

"I don't like reality much I guess."

Mario was thoughtful for a moment. Then he said, "La verita, uccidera. Always remember that."

Carol laughed. "What does it mean?"

"The truth will kill you."

"I believe that!"

"It's good to be a seeker of truth, Carol," Mario said. "It just doesn't pay well." He got up and started to clear things away.

"I'm a good dishwasher," Carol said, taking the plates out of his hands. "I'll take care of everything."

"That's right. I remember. Lots of soap. A good worker."

Carol was embarrassed, but she said "Thanks, Mario," and realized she had much more to thank him for. "Mario, I don't know why you're helping me, but thank you very much."

"Why shouldn't I help a friend? It's nothing. I'll be back in the morning. There's some juice and bread and cheese in the refrigerator. I'll bring something for breakfast. Get some sleep. Don't worry about anything. Okay?"

"Okay," Carol said, and she meant it. As soon as the dishes were done, Carol unpacked her small suitcase, brushed her teeth, put on her pajamas and made up the bed with the fresh white sheets Mario had left for her. She was tired. She turned out the light and went right to sleep.

CHAPTER FOURTEEN

Velvickia

Brigid," Orion laughed softly and sat up on her elbow, "are you all right? I didn't hurt you?"

Brigid lay still, her eyes closed. "Just enough," she said, opening her eyes and smiling. She looked at Orion for a moment. "Are you sure Dierdra's been the only other woman in your life?"

"Yes."

"Then you've made beautiful love to yourself." She was thoughtful for a moment. "Do you know that you talk to yourself?"

"Yeah, I know."

"You've been alone too long, my love."

"You know, I didn't know it till I had someone to talk to. That started at Pinecliff, and it happened again here this last week with the other women. They know what I mean before I even finish my sentence."

Brigid laughed. "Sometimes it's spooky, but, yeah, it's a relief to not have to explain everything."

"Men don't seem to want to understand."

"They don't think they can afford to. You know, they're really hard on each other."

"Yeah, I guess I do know that, but you probably know it better, working with them all day."

"Thank God I don't have to sleep with them."

Here Orion closed her eyes. "Oh, Brigid."

"What?"

When Orion opened her eyes, Brigid saw there were tears in them.

"Until now, until…making love, being in love with you…I didn't know how lonely I was all these years."

Brigid took Orion into her arms. "I'm here now. I'm here."

*   *   *   *   *

The days passed, and even though Orion was tired almost every one of those days from not getting enough sleep, she had more energy and more ideas for her work than she had ever had before. Shapes and images and new ways of mixing colors, making them bright, came to her so fast at times they crowded in on each other and had to be sorted and looked at and then played with, one by one, till the most persistent found their way onto the canvas.

And every night, love. Being known, knowing. Trying not even to wish it would never end so that the end would not be thought of at all.

Santa Cruz was making an effort to revive itself. The main

street had been closed off to traffic and made into a pedestrian walkway with wooden benches and small fountains inviting shoppers to sit awhile. Many of the shops and restaurants were new, but there were still plenty of old businesses and mom and pop coffee shops.

Down at the beach, the boardwalk had been rebuilt and the roller coaster completely overhauled. The old hotel had just reopened, palm trees in heavy expensive Chinese pots at the entrance and throughout the large old rooms, velvet drapes on the floor to ceiling lead glass windows, crystal chandeliers, hardwood floors—everything just right for Saturday night ballroom dance competitions and afternoon tea. They served brunch in the dining room till three on weekends.

It was Saturday. Tomorrow the last day. Orion and Brigid had decided the night before to go to brunch at the old hotel and talk about Sunday, talk about the future. They wouldn't have to be back till seven when there would be a final group meeting and exhibition of what they'd done during the two weeks. Brigid's piece was already up. The tangles of seals had worked up to a series of elongated disks, the shapes evolving, moving into each other in smooth fluid movements. She called it "Balancing Act." Orion wasn't sure if she'd show her things. They were so new and different. She'd been assigned a space, though, and she still had time to hang them if she wanted to.

Saturday morning before the sun rose Brigid and Orion awoke making love that was fierce and wordless. Then they spoke briefly about what time they should get up and what they would need to do that day. Then they fell back asleep.

When they woke the second time there was a desert, vast and frightening between them. Brigid had stayed at Orion's so

she left to shower and change, and when she did Orion felt, for
the first time, what her absence was going to mean to her. She
thought of the desert flower Father John had described to the
class once. It was somewhere in Africa that it grew, somewhere
on the Sahara, she thought. It was dormant, came to life once
in a thousand years—maybe it was a hundred—when there was
sufficient rain upon it for a long enough period of time, a few
hours maybe. Then it would spring open, gigantic, full and
beautiful for just a day or two. Then it closed again, dry and
dead looking till the next time, decades, long years later. She
would look in an encyclopedia and find the name of that flower
and a good photo of it, too, and then she'd paint it, a mile high
painting, full of every color she could conceive of belonging to
such a flower. and paint it.

Throughout the meal, the women were either quiet or both
talking at once. They weren't hungry but they tried to eat and
even went back for more, adding something, anything, sitting
back down, talking but not talking.

Finally Brigid pointed to the chocolate mousse in front of
Orion and said, "Are you going to eat that?"

"No."

"Let's go then. Let's go down to the sand dunes."

Orion looked at her watch.

"We have time. I'll help you put your paintings up."

"I know. I just don't want to have this conversation."

"It might be easier looking out at the sea."

When they got to the dunes, the sky had become overcast,
and the sea breeze was strong. The two women bundled up in
their jackets and scarves, their hands in their pockets as they
walked onto the sand.

"There," Orion said, pointing to a spot surrounded by tall grasses. They stretched out, side by side, and looked down to the sea.

A little girl was there, playing. She had a white ruffled dress on and she was running as fast as she could, screaming and howling at the sea as it withdrew, then turning and running away from it as it advanced.

"She knows when to chase it," Orion said, laughing.

"And when to run away."

Orion started to respond but just then a man and a woman passed them on the dunes, calling down to the little girl. She didn't seem to hear them. The women watched as the girl finally turned and saw her parents, as she reluctantly walked toward them, as her mother put a jacket on her, as her father swept her up in his arms, as they started up the shoreline and then turned out of sight.

"Brigid, just let me hold you. Let's not talk yet."

Brigid shook her head, but then she smiled and moved into Orion's arms and they looked out at the sea in silence.

*   *   *   *   *

When Carol got back home, she went straight for Mrs. Martin's booze. She tried to keep it locked up but was usually too looped or too hung over to do anything right. Carol took out a big bottle of gin and a big bottle of whiskey. She opened the whiskey and drank some. The she flew out the door and back up the alley.

"Rufus! Rufus!"

He saw her, but he didn't respond till he realized what she

had in her hands. "Hey, child, what you doing with them bottles?"

"Giving them to you. Paying you back. And Fanny. Where's Fanny?"

"Don't worry. She be back," he said, his hand reaching for the whiskey, taking a sip. "You can wait here or leave that gin. I give it to her."

"Yeah. You give it to her. Tell her I brang it. Okay?"

"Maybe you better wait here. You fixing to have another fit?"

"Yes, Rufus, I am."

Rufus laughed. "They going to put you away."

"I don't care."

"Well, here then," he said, handing the whiskey back to her. "You need some fire under that."

Carol took the whiskey back and let the fire enter and build and fill her up with anger and some kind of protection for what she figured would happen when Mrs. Martin found out her booze was gone.

"You thief! You lying thief!" Mrs. Martin was home. One of her scruffy boyfriends was with her.

"I didn't lie. I told you I took it."

"Don't you talk to Mrs. Martin like that!" The boyfriend said, and Carol heard his words slur. He was drunk and moving quickly toward her, his fist raised.

Carol found herself on the floor, her ears ringing. Then she felt a kick in her stomach—a woman's pointy shoe or a cowboy boot. Was he wearing boots? She looked up and saw it was Mrs. Martin's foot coming at her for a second time. She grabbed her ankle and pulled her off balance. Mrs. Martin fell back, away from her and then she just lay there, still.

"My God," the boyfriend yelled, "you've killed her."

Carol stood up and went over to Mrs. Martin. She didn't look dead. Carol got some water and threw it on her while the boyfriend tried to revive her by slapping her face. Carol tried to seize the moment and run past him and out of the door, but he caught her from behind in a bear hug. Carol kicked him in the shins as hard as she could.

"Goddamn you little bitch," he yelled in pain, but he didn't let her go. "I'll get you for that!" Suddenly there was a call at the front door.

"Carol! Carol you in there?" It was Fanny.

"Fanny! Fanny! Help me!" The boyfriend put his hand over Carol's mouth and strengthened his hold on her further down so that she couldn't kick him very well. With what seemed like lightning speed, he got Carol and himself across the room, into the bedroom, and down into a corner of the closet. Carol heard Fanny again, but this time it was a scream.

"Help! Rufus come here." Then Carol could hear Mrs. Martin's voice.

"It's all right. Don't worry. I'm okay. I just fell down."

"Oh, I thought I heard Carol calling out."

"No. She's not here. She's at school."

"Oh. Yes, ma'm. Okay."

Carol felt the boyfriend's hand go into her panties, and she heard him say, "You ain't never been fucked have you girlie?" His other hand had loosened over her mouth, and Carol bit into it with the strength she had. Again he swore at her, but this time he let her loose and then he smacked her across the face with the back of his hand and she felt something go crack in her neck as she hit the wall of the closet.

"You in there, Zeke?"

"Yeah, baby. Got your little wild cat in here, teaching her a thing or two." The door opened and Mrs. Martin stood, still woozy from the fall, but her eyes full of evil intent.

"Let me have a swat at her."

The boyfriend stood outside the door. "Have all you want," he smiled, "I'll be here to make sure she don't try nothing with you."

Mrs. Martin didn't try to kick this time. She grabbed a broom that was by the door and started poking it at Carol, but it wasn't hitting its mark.

"Here, honey. Let me help you," Zeke said, taking off his belt. "This'll be easier. I'll show you how it's done." He struck Carol with the belt right across her face, and Carol felt herself go numb and not there, but watching. She saw him hand the belt to Mrs. Martin. Again the belt across her face. But no pain. No pain at all, and no tears. Nothing.

"She won't even cry, Zeke. That girl's not repentant, you know. She's just evil."

"Here, give me that." Zeke took the belt and whipped Carol for what seemed like a long time. Finally she fell to her knees. He stepped back. Mrs. Martin stepped in and started slapping Carol with the back of her hand and then the front. Then she kicked her in the chest.

"I can show her evil if you want me to, honey." Carol heard Zeke unzip his pants.

That stopped her. That stopped Mrs. Martin. "Hey," she said in a quiet voice, "what are you talking about? That's enough. That's enough. Let's go get a drink." He didn't want to stop, but he wasn't going to go on without Mrs. Martin being part of it. Reluctantly, he zipped his pants back up, keeping his belt in his hand, giving her looks. Then Mrs. Martin pushed Carol back further into the closet. They closed the door and locked it, and Carol passed out on the floor.

*   *   *   *   *

Sunday. Orion was on the coast road going home. They shook hands. Brigid and Orion shook hands and said goodbye. They had let the future go and each other go. They shook hands. Brigid said, "If you want to make a big decision, call me. If you just want to see me for the night or the afternoon, I won't do it. I knew that before I came down here and I felt it strongly yesterday when we woke up the second time."

"I felt it, too." Orion looked away for a moment. "I'm not as brave as you are."

"You are, Orion. Anyway, I'm not as brave as you think I am. I was never attracted to men. I couldn't possibly have married one."

"Brigid, you don't know how many women marry men they are not at all attracted to. You don't even know why they do."

"Sure I do. It's fear. Well, I have another kind of fear. I know I can earn enough money to have the things I want, do the things I want to do. But I am afraid of hooking up with a woman who's having a fling. If I let you, you'll play me out on this…"

"I'm not playing."

"Sorry. I didn't mean that. I meant… remember what I said on the bridge—my policy statements?"

"Yeah."

"That's what I mean. It hurts me personally and it hurts women like me politically—though I'll have to say I'm not thinking so much of that right now. I can't let myself get caught up in a situation I see as just plain wrong. I won't be the other woman. I won't wait by the phone. I won't talk you into anything either. You do what's right for you, Orion.

"Brigid, I'm in love with you."

"Orion, you know how I feel, but there's something so important to me—self-respect. I have to feel that for myself. I fear anything that might make me lose that. If I let this situation slide….One more thing. If you ever want to get things straight and clear, you got to stay sober, Orion. For a long time."

"If I'd had any idea that not drinking was going to bring all this on, I don't think I'd have ever stopped."

They smiled at each other for the first time that morning.

"I don't believe you regret a minute," Brigid said.

"I don't," Orion allowed. "I'm going to try to stay sober for a while. See how bad things can get." They laughed and they embraced for just a second, like good friends. Then they shook hands. And that was that.

Frank was happy to see her. He opened the door and then opened his arms. She moved forward into those arms and there she was stopped. The wall. She had her arms around a wall. But this was home, and as soon as she stepped into it, she was sure this was what she had to have. She needed this place and this history—her only history with another human being—and normalcy. This was a normal life. Husband and house and a history. Out there was quicksand.

"Hey, don't tell me you didn't miss me," he said, almost

coyly as he took a step back away from her. "I made dinner. Spaghetti." Frank took Orion's suitcase. "I'll help you get the rest out later."

"Okay. I'd like you to see what…."

"I tried to make the sauce like you do, but I think I didn't put enough spices in it."

"I'm not quite ready for dinner. I did stop on the way up."

"You did? Didn't you think we might have dinner together?"

"I mentioned it on the phone."

"Yeah? Well, the table's set. Think I'll go ahead. I'm starving. Do you mind?"

Orion shook her head. "No, and that'll give me a chance to bring some of my paintings in. Would you like…."

"That spaghetti's going to be good. And I've got a pitcher of martinis—don't worry, no ice melting in the gin. In the freezer."

"Thanks, honey. I'll go get my things. Go ahead. I'll have some a little later."

"Okay," he said and tried to blow her a kiss. Then it all started again. Frank trying to blow her a kiss, his lips smacking apart like his mouth had, with effort, unhinged for a second and then a gust of air from the throat, clearing the throat. Was that a kiss blown? Anger started up in her chest, but she didn't know why or at whom she was angry. It felt wrong. Just as quickly as everything had felt right, it now felt wrong.

Orion turned and ran down the stairs to the car. Her hand was trembling so hard she couldn't squeeze the handle on the door. She leaned against the car and looked up at the kitchen window where Frank was busy doing something. It was odd seeing him in the kitchen, even seeing him home and her outside the home. It's his home, she thought. His.

Orion steadied herself, opened the car door and got in behind the driver's seat. "My car," she said. "I paid for this car." But he paid for the insurance and the maintenance and repair. Even if divorce was possible, even if half is hers, she didn't earn it, she didn't make anything happen at all. All she had done was marry.

She hit the steering column and accidentally hit the horn. Frank looked up, out the window at her. She honked again and then continued to honk, banging her fist repeatedly on the horn till Frank ran down the stairs and pulled her away from the car and back into the house. Orion ran down the stairs to their bedroom and closed the door. Frank did not follow.

*   *   *   *   *

Orion had taken a long bath and then gone to lie down. It was an hour before Frank came into the bedroom. Orion saw his face was drawn and blotchy as if he'd nearly cried. The worry on his face touched her and shamed her.

"Frank, I'm sorry. Please give me a little time. I just need some time."

"You just had two weeks, Carol."

"Orion," she whispered.

Frank sighed and shook his head. "That's another thing. I swear I don't know who you are anymore." They looked at each other, and Orion felt her face burn with shame. Why couldn't she be the way she had been or at least seem to be the way she had seemed to be? She couldn't bear his gaze. Had he never looked at her before, into her eyes? Had she sought his? Had she hidden? Why was she ashamed?

"I am so sorry."

"Try to figure out what's going on. Maybe you should see a therapist or someone."

"Maybe we could go together."

"There's nothing wrong with me, Ca…Orion." Frank sighed again. "This all started when you stopped drinking. Maybe you should just cut down, you know." A heavier sigh. "I've got work to do." He left the door open to his office, and Orion could hear him turn the computer on. Soon she heard him clicking away. She listened to the clicks for a minute or two. She found she was holding her breath, that she couldn't seem to breathe. She felt panic rising in her and she forced herself to exhale and then inhale deeply and then blow the breath out of herself. She saw Frank blowing her his kiss. She had to do something. She moved quickly out of bed and started up the stairs. Halfway up, she stopped, sat down, wanted to think, her legs spread upon the granite rock, sun-bathed, Brigid's kisses coming from deep inside her passing everything she had ever wanted, had always wanted, up through her body to her lips to Orion's open legs and to her heart, to her heart that filled to bursting. She popped up, ran the rest of the way up the stairs and came to an abrupt halt, landing in the kitchen. A drink, wholly wanting a drink, wanting nothing else. No feelings, no thoughts, nothing.

She opened the freezer door. The pitcher was there, frosted. So was the martini glass. She took the pitcher in both hands and put it on the kitchen counter. She took the glass and closed the freezer door. She turned and leaned against the refrigerator, glass in hand and looked across at the pitcher of gin and vermouth. Three to one he made them. It would be oily. She couldn't remember where she'd hidden the gin in the kitchen. She didn't want to go to the bar. He would hear her. He would know she was putting more gin in the martini. He would come up. He would blow her a kiss. A blow to the head. A cowboy boot or pointy shoes. What was the point? Get to the point. She crossed the floor passed Dierdra and Mother Superior. There was no one on the other side. She wanted to cry for someone to come. Mother Superior, mother. Someone. Some help had to be coming from somewhere. "Father John!" she said his name out loud. She heard Frank come to the bottom of the stairs, and she stood as still as she could until she heard him go back into the office. She couldn't hear the clicks but she knew that by now he was clicking and his jaw was clamped shut, as it always was except for when he tried to make kisses. It was clamped shut now and that was better.

She poured herself a drink only to find she couldn't raise the glass. Her hand was shaking and the glass was so light. She couldn't breathe again. She exhaled and inhaled. Then she braced her two hands against the kitchen counter and bent over the drink to sip the drink, but she couldn't hold her head steady either. She raised herself up and tried again to breathe, to exhale and then inhale. She felt the sweat dripping down her face. Those weren't tears she was sure. She put both hands on the pitcher. It was heavy. She could drink from this heavy pitcher. It didn't shake very much at all. She raised it, but then, betrayal, it started to shake as if the gin itself was causing it to shake and she couldn't control it. It was like a jackhammer in her hands.

The pitcher started to pull away from her. She couldn't hold it back, and when she released it, it flew across the room, crashing against the refrigerator. The pieces fell in very slow motion, one piece and then one other piece and then all of them raining down, hitting the floor, jumping and flying and then Frank's footsteps coming up the stairs.

"What happened? What broke? My God. Did you throw it?"

"I don't know. Frank, help me."

"I'll get a broom."

"No. Help me!"

"What are you talking about? What the hell's wrong with you?"

"I don't know."

"I'm calling a doctor."

"Yes. All right. Put me downstairs. Lock the door."

"Lock the…." Frank went to the phone, checked the code for the doctor he had programmed into the system. Couldn't find it. He was upset. He called information. It was busy, a recording or something. He banged the phone down and found the phone book. He found the number. He punched it in. He got a recording. He pressed a number. Then another number. He spoke into the answering machine. When he looked up he saw that Orion had fainted.

CHAPTER FIFTEEN

The Note

Parrots wake her. Not their sound. Their color. Wake her. Acrylic feathers, blue, green, red, wings moving, at first soundlessly, wake her.

Before she hears the birds, other sounds reach her. She hears the breeze moving through bamboo in a low lazy whistle. Mimosa branches, too, play upon the movement, tentatively, fingers shy upon a harp soft breeze. She sees flowers, larger than melons, crepe paper colors of indigo and fuchsia, colors that beam, lending light to the quiet vitality of pale pink and soft yellow on the smaller flowers that are spread freely throughout the low lying grasses.

Carp, speckled and gold come shimmering to the edge of the pond. Lime green algae brightens the shade on the far side of the pond; on this side, where the carp swim, the algae floats pale upon the water. The carp nibble at it, lips distinctly marked, opening and closing in a silent chorus of Cambrian chants.

There is moss overhead, chartreuse, and orchids, purple and yellow, clinging, nesting, flowing from the dark green canopy of the trees. And now the parrots can be heard as they perch and puff their body-warm talk in the treetops. Their voices grow stronger.

The girl, a small blonde child, moves through the park, to its edge, and finds herself at the top of a muddy embankment. Tall grasses, taller than she is, crowd the open water before her. All is still now, the brown water, the grass, the pale blue sky.

A man, naked except for a G-string, moves into her vision. He is calm, easy, relaxed in an animal comfort with nature. He sits on a canoe with an oar and a spear. He doesn't speak, seems never to have had a need to speak, but he laughs playfully, beckoning her to join him. He will take her through the tall grasses to the open lake. He wants to go, but she is filled with uncertainty.

An aroma of something baking wafts over her. It smells of yeast and honey. She turns away from the man in the canoe and moves toward the source of the aroma, following it into the trees which are now pines that quickly open to a valley.

It is snowing steadily, softly. The baking must be going on in that cabin down below. Suddenly, she is in the cabin, in the living room, a fire is burning in the fireplace. She's wearing pajamas and is wrapped warmly in a thick quilt. A man is sitting on the rocking chair a few feet away from her. She is safe.

There is a noise outside the window. The man turns and looks over her shoulder to see what's going on. He says "It's all right. I'll take care of it," and the girl believes it is all right and he will take care of it.

He goes out. There is someone there, lurking. He sees it is a woman, but it is not a reasoning woman; it's a predator with only the instinct to have in its mouth the flesh that will sustain its life. It is in the shadows, moving listlessly in the shadows, shielding itself from the lights coming from the kitchen. The man knows he cannot talk to the predator. No words will reach her. She must simply be exterminated. He puts one arm around her and talks soothingly into her ear. In his free hand he has a gun with a silencer on it. As he talks, he moves the gun to her belly and shoots her. Then he takes off his jacket, digs a grave and buries her in the snow.

He returns to the room. There's sadness here now. The girl is safe, but the brightness has dimmed.

Strudel. That's what the woman in the kitchen was baking. She is not the man's wife, but his housekeeper. She is a little like the predator, but with more reasoning power. She knows the rules, respects authority, does what she is told, and often takes the initiative, but she is his servant and sometimes needs to be reminded of her place. She tsks tsks, thinks the man is a bit off, not quite what he should be, not quite what she would be if their roles were reversed. She would not stew over things the way he does. Too much compunction can stop you in your tracks.

The woman is fussing in the kitchen with the strudel. The man goes back outside to check on the grave. The girl slips unnoticed into the kitchen and sees a note pad on the table. There's something written on the top sheet. She takes it into her hands and slides under the table, disappears into the half-light that makes its way through the linen tablecloth, now her enclosure. She sits comfortably upon the floor, leans for just a moment against a table leg; then is jolted forward by what she knows even before she puts the letters together to form the words. The note is printed in the sharp sure letters of a draftsman. She looks at the letters of the words again, trying to make them say something else, but she can't.

She shuts her eyes tight to protect herself from understanding, but she sees the words anyway. Printed in a clear orderly hand. In capital letters. Three words: "KILL THE GIRL."

CHAPTER SIXTEEN

Well, She Was Not Dead

Her eyes were nearly swollen shut, but Carol was able to see that there was light coming in from under the door. A faint bit of light was coming in through the keyhole, too. Had they tried to kill her? Well, she was not dead.

Slowly, she got to her knees, but when she looked through the keyhole, she found there was something blocking her view. For a second she wondered if her eye had been damaged, but quickly she realized it was the key still in the keyhole. She listened for a long time. It was quiet. They must have gone out. Slowly she turned the doorknob. The door was locked.

Carol listened again for a while. Then she reached up in the dark and found a coat hanger, unwound the neck and poked one end through the keyhole. She heard the key fall to the floor. "Stupid," she started to say, but found she couldn't quite form the word and she thought, 'Maybe I'll look like a monster now for the rest of my life.' She let the thought go.

How was she going to get the key? She leaned forward to position herself on the floor, but a stabbing pain in her ribs thrust her back. She tried again more slowly and found she could stay ahead of the pain if she just continued to move very carefully, but when she finally got herself flat on the floor, she felt again the pain and nearly cried out. She waited till it passed. Then she took a deep breath and held it as she pressed her swollen face against the floor. She saw the key wasn't far from her.

She lay there, still, trying to breathe normally. Then she took in another deep breath and, keeping her body as still as possible, she felt around the floor of the closet for another hanger and quickly found one. She fed the hanger out and looped an end over the key, but the wire was too thin and slippery, the key too big and full of notches. She brought the hanger back into the closet, slowly turned over on her back and felt some relief in her chest. She tried to look around to get an idea of what she could use to get the key, but she really couldn't see well enough. Then she remembered she still had her school shoes on—she could use the laces.

This time, she brought her foot toward her hands. The pain was more tolerable on her back. She untied one shoelace and drew it out. When the lace was free, she carefully wound it around the coat hanger, knotting it as she went.

When that work was done, she had the harder slower work of turning over onto her belly. It seemed to take her forever and when she finally made it, she had to stop and rest. She tried again for the key. This time when she looped the key, it came forward without a hitch. She was drawing it in when she heard a hard knocking at the front door. For a second she froze. Then in one sure movement, she brought the key into the closet.

"Carol? Carol? Mrs. Martin?" It was a man's voice. A white man, but he sounded sober and not like someone who'd go out with Mrs. Martin. She heard the screen door open. Then a thump. Someone was breaking in. Heavy footsteps. More than one person. Maybe they wouldn't try the closet. In what seemed like an instant, they were at the door, banging on the closet door.

"Carol? Are you in there?" They tried the door again. Then she heard a woman's voice.

"Carol, honey. It's the police come to get you."

"Panny!" her lips allowed.

"Yes, honey."

"Stand away from the door!"

Carol moved back. "I'b got da...key," she started to say, but they had the pulled the door open before she finished her sentence.

Bright light blasted in at her and everything looked blurry. She squinted through her swollen lids and saw two policemen standing in front of her, Fanny just behind trying to see past them.

"It's all right, baby. Come on out. Oh, Lord, what they do to you? Come here child." Carol went to Fanny, and she let herself be held, but everything hurt and they could all see that it did.

"We'll take you to a hospital Carol," one of the policemen said. "Then we'll see what Social Services wants to do."

"Call Bader John...Immaculada." Carol mumbled. "Dell him come see me."

"Okay," he said, but Carol wasn't sure if he meant it, and she wouldn't move forward with him. She stood and looked, as best she could, into his eyes. "I promise," he said, and she believed him. "Now, let's go."

"Go on child. They here to help. It going be all right now." Fanny patted Carol lightly on her shoulder, afraid she might hurt her."

"You knew?"

Fanny nodded. "Don't rightly know how, but I knew. Came by to say thank you for your little present. I could feel something was wrong. I had a time getting the police to believe me, but this one," she looked at the officer who had promised to call Father John, "why he was sent by the Lord to cruise right by here and when I went up to the car, why he listened. He said, 'Yes ma'm, we'll follow you,' and he followed me right here. You okay now, honey. You go on with the police. They take care of you." Fanny looked at the young policeman, searching out his intention on his face. He nodded to Fanny and said to Carol, "That's right. We're going to take care of you. You are safe now." Safe. The word felt like a hurricane blown in her ear. It swirled into her head and started revolving. Safe. Carol felt her legs grow weak and started to collapse, but Fanny caught her on one side, the policeman on the other. They walked her out to the police car like that.

Carol's eyes registered the flashing red and blue lights. She was aware, more by sound than sight, that there was a crush of people there too. Seemed like the whole neighborhood was there. Federico tried to talk to her, but the policeman stopped him, stopped anyone from talking to her as he carefully placed her in the back of the car. She heard the siren start and they drove off.

CHAPTER SEVENTEEN

All the Names

When she came to, Frank and the doctor, blurred, were looking down at her, swinging over her like a pendulum. She closed her eyes against the movement.

The next time she opened her eyes, she was alone in the bedroom and it was light out. She looked across at the hydrangea that grew wild on the hill just outside the sliding glass doors. They were pale blue, almost white, beautiful against the sparse tall grasses and brown earth. She had seen the flowers a hundred times before. She wanted to see them a hundred times again.

On clear days, she could see the stacked white and pastel houses of Noe Valley and across the bay to the Berkeley Hills. She wondered, this morning, if those hills were part of the same range that ran down to San Jose, if they joined the Santa Cruz Mountains. If she would ever see Brigid again. She looked at the phone, noticed there was a note next to it. A note. What had she dreamed? Something terrible? Never mind. It didn't matter. Being awake was terror enough. "Terror?" she asked herself. She shook her head, reached for the note and read, "I'll stop by at noon and see if you're awake. Take it easy. Frank."

Yes. That was it. Take it easy. Never mind the dream. Never mind anything at all. She leaned back on her pillow, closed her eyes and once again fell asleep.

The third time it was the afternoon sun that woke her. It came slanting in from the high windows above their bed and reflected off the glass doors right into her eyes.

There was another note: "You were asleep. I figured you needed it. See you later. Frank."

Orion looked at Frank's handwriting. It was neat, easy to read, slanting gently to the right. Exactly like him. Maybe there was nothing more, nothing deeper. And he seemed to be happy enough playing sports, playing games, reading the paper. It never upset him to read the paper. In fact, it relaxed him—no matter what the news was. Why couldn't she be happy like that? Hadn't she been? Couldn't she just leave things alone now and return to the way things were?

No. She wanted to understand.

Understand what?

Something she was close to naming when she was in Santa Cruz, something she experienced sometimes when she was painting and sometimes when she was with Brigid—in silence with Brigid. Somehow she was being drawn closer to something not known through words.

Manassas, Antietam, Gettysburg, Shiloh, Vicksburg, Sherman marching through Georgia. Frank did talk. About facts, more or less recited them, so she was learning them too. He knew all the battles of the Civil War. He even knew the names of all the American Presidents and sometimes recited them to her. Why did she listen? Sit there and listen? Because he was, at least, saying something. There were words coming from him to her. It vaguely informed her about him, at least she knew what facts were on his mind. He had invited her more than once to go with him on his yearly trips to re-enact Civil War battles. He had uniforms and muskets. She had never gone. She would have to witness it, and she was afraid she would laugh or find a real gun and shoot him. She didn't know why.

What did they learn from these exercises? It was one bloody event after the next, whatever the heroism. Nothing changed. No, the characters changed. So did the time, the fashions, the technology.

The world wide web. He clicks away at it endlessly. An infinity of information to get lost in, strands connecting with the speed of light, but always still, never acknowledging the movement of the spider.

Digicide.

Kill the girl. Was she dead?

You are nothing. Then I did not live and I did not die. Nothing at all.

"Jesus," she said. "Jesus Christ!" Orion crumpled Frank's note and held it in her fist as she got out of bed. She was going to do something. What was it? She could call Brigid. And say what? She lay back down.

Once more she closed her eyes. She didn't want to open them again till she was sure there would be out there a scene she could take for granted. She didn't want to notice the mums or the hills or the sky or any of the battle or even any heroes. She didn't want to see or hear or be aware of anything. She needed a drink.

CHAPTER EIGHTEEN

Betrayed, Part II

Orion did not want a drink. She didn't even want to sleep. There was no sleep left in her. There was love, there was longing, there was passion. Orion got up quickly and left the bedroom. She went to her studio, and she dialed Brigid's number.

"Hello."

"Brigid?"

"Hello. How are you?"

"Brigid, this is Orion."

"Yes. How are you? What a surprise to hear from you."

Orion was silent. Something was wrong. She tried to steady herself.

"Brigid, this is Orion."

"Hold on a minute." Orion heard Brigid cover the phone with her hand. She was speaking to someone.

"Orion?"

"Yes."

"Can I call you back in a few minutes? Someone's here."

Orion waited.

"I'm sorry. I really didn't expect to hear from you."

"I didn't expect to call," Orion felt the life drain out of her.

Silence.

"Orion?"

Her voice was already steel when she found it again. "Brigid, it doesn't matter."

"It matters to me. Come on. Let's meet. Meet me somewhere in an hour or later on."

Orion didn't speak.

"Tomorrow?"

A woman's voice called Brigid's name. Again Brigid muffled the phone, spoke to whoever it was and returned.

"Orion? Orion, I am sorry you happened to call at this particular time, but really, I didn't know if I'd ever hear from you again."

Orion remained silent.

"Be fair. We made no plans, and certainly we made no commitments."

Orion felt anger pulling her away from safety, bringing her back to chaos. "We won't be making any plans, either. Not for tomorrow. Not for any time." No. She would not be angry. She would be safe. "I'm sorry, too, Brigid, but I won't be calling again, and please don't call me."

"Do you mean that?"

"Yes."

Orion did not slam the phone down. She did not have tears in her eyes or even in her throat. She was thirsty. That was all.

She headed for the kitchen. She would have a drink.

As she made her way up the stairs she determined that she would return to her life with Frank. She would be, again, a normal woman with a normal man. She would have a normal life. Cocktails. She would be happy.

When she got to the top of the stairs, Orion saw that Frank's briefcase was on the kitchen table. He was home. She hadn't heard him come in. "Frank?"

Frank was standing, the kitchen phone in his hand, his face tight and red, his hard set mouth pressed down and flat.

"What was that?" he asked.

Orion felt the room begin to turn. She sat down at the kitchen table. But even as she did, she knew the table was not there, nor the kitchen, nor Frank. The house was gone. She had lost her home, lost her place. She was out, again, alone, floating in space.

"You're a freak!" Frank yelled.

Orion had never heard Frank yell before. It surprised her. She nearly smiled.

"You're a freak!" he yelled again, and Orion, in spite of the storming confusion in her head, experienced tremendous pleasure that Frank was angry, connected to her, engaged. And, in the next moment, came the sharp understanding that it was this very engagement that would make him turn away from her. Frank had a heart. It could be broken. But he would not allow it.

Softly she said, "Maybe I am a freak, Frank, but what's funny is that I see now you're not." She looked into his bewildered eyes, into the hurt and shock in his eyes, and for the first time she felt love for him. "I am so sorry that this is what it took for me to see you."

"What're you talking about?" He was more confused than angry now. Soon he would be merely disappointed. Soon he would tell himself that he did not have to put up with this kind of behavior. There was the drinking and then the police. Now this. No, it was too much. He was a civilized person, and, my god, hadn't he taken her in? She wasn't making any money teaching art. She was no artist to begin with. Those squiggles. And she wasn't even that good of a weekend mother to his kids. It was a mistake. It was all a mistake. How could he have chosen her to be his wife? How could he have made such a mistake? He was too softhearted. That was his problem. He couldn't really be blamed, though. He wouldn't be.

Orion knew all this as she sat at the table and heard Frank say, "Now what are we going to do?"

What she did not know was that he had loved her, even though he didn't know her. Indeed, it was the only way he could love.

He had felt there was something strange, even menacing, about her, something waiting to show itself. He had not suspected it was this. This unnatural thing. Here in his house. Oh, he didn't want to think about it. It was just awful. That's all. She had definitely crossed the line. That was it. He would take no more.

What she didn't know was that Frank would find someone who would tell him he was perfect, that he was indeed blameless, that he had done all a man could do and more. What she didn't know was that together he and that someone would bury his love for her and his errors and his shame. They would set their respective jaws, and they would be happy.

For her this glimpse of love for him, coming as it did at the moment of loss, and the loss of her, too, coming as it did just moments before—the juncture of love and loss and love and loss would open pathways for everything and everyone she had ever buried.

They would all come treading the dark artery opened in her infancy, opened that silent and sudden moment when she realized it was useless to set her mouth for mother's milk.

Even as she sat at the kitchen table, she felt the specters stir, the woman, the man, the girl, the boy, the foster parents and the foster brothers and sisters, the children who ran in and out of the house that was theirs.

Every love and every loss, she would feel in every layer of skin and every twisting sinew and in some eternal place that knows outrage before it knows language. The incisions and extractions, all of it, she would feel.

Far more painful than the rest, she would know shame. Not shame the way Frank knew it, not guilty of human error, or even the shame he would expect her to feel over loving another woman—which she would never feel—but profound shame, shame of her very nature, the odious nature that she had been born with that no baptism or absolution had managed to exorcise, a nature so loathsome that even people who had wanted to love her, could not.

And, although she was not conscious of it, she made a decision, sitting there at the kitchen table, that she would know all of this and feel all of this, that this time she would find the strength not to resist. She would admit in her pulses and on her trembling lips every betrayal and abandonment since the first one.

She would not have a drink. She would go unanesthetized

into this knowledge, and if she died from it, she died. If she didn't, she would live. She would not be a zombie.

Unknown mother, unknown father, and all that she had known who had pushed her away or from whom she had, unremittingly been separated—they would come now, risen, to accuse and embrace her.

But she couldn't remember them in thought and not in images either. So this man—who was now turning away, he who had made a vow never ever to do that—he would wear the cloak and the shroud that had kept love hidden from her for as long as she could remember and even before that, especially before that.

So every step he took to hide and protect himself from her, she would feel as every step ever taken away from her. And she would rail against him, howl and scream, and he would be astonished and terrified. And so would she.

"Well," he repeated, "what are we going to do?"

CHAPTER NINETEEN

Who Knows?
Who Cares?

For a minute, as she lay there in the dark, Carol couldn't remember where she was.

"Mario," she said as she remembered him. Dierdra. Crazy Denise. Her life now, again, completely changed. Their lives? Who knows? Why care? She got up, felt for the light and flicked it on. The clock said it was eight. She had been asleep for almost six hours. She flicked the light back off and sat on the edge of the bed. For the first time in her life, she was not afraid of the dark; in fact, it soothed her. She didn't quite have the words, but she saw the image—light, it was light, burning light that was dangerous. She would stay like this, in the dark, for as long as she could.

When Mario came, he saw that she had changed. She was calm, but in a way that told him she was defeated. He tried to attribute it to the shock of what she'd just been through, or maybe to an accumulation of the many shocks she'd had in her young life, but he couldn't be sure.

"Carol, I have a sister in Sacramento. She's older than me, an old woman, but she would take you in. You could help her with errands, stuff like that."

"Did you talk to her already?"

Mario nodded. "She's a nice woman. She won't hurt you. I'd see you, too, at the holidays, Christmas, Easter."

"Sure, Mario. That would be nice. When do I go?"

"I think the sooner the better."

"Okay. Let's just go then. Let's go."

Mario watched Carol as she spoke. She seemed to be talking herself into it. She seemed forlorn. He would have taken her in his arms, but he was sure that would scare her.

"Okay. Let's go."

Mario took Carol downtown to the bus station. It would be a long ride, the bus stopping in every town between Los Angeles and San Francisco, thirteen hours or so. Mario packed her breakfast, lunch and dinner. The bag was nearly as big as her suitcase. It did, at least, make her smile a little when she saw it. She smiled again as the bus pulled out and she waved goodbye. Mario had never seen her looking so sad.

When the holidays had come and he'd gone to see his sister and Carol, he saw that she had not gotten her old self back. Well, maybe she never would. But she had a nice place to live, she was going to high school, getting B's and C's and that was okay. Sometimes she got A's in Art. She was working after school in a Mexican restaurant. She stopped waitressing when she started college at San Francisco State, where she was made a Teaching

Assistant. It paid less, but it was better for her career. She was serious about everything, somber even. She didn't have any close friends, and she didn't seem to care for the things most young women cared about—clothes, going to dances, boys. She didn't seem to notice trends, what was in fashion. She was simple in her dress and in her needs. The only thing that she seemed to really enjoy was making her drawings, ink and brush. They were good, Mario could see, but they were subdued. Something or someone would have to find the spark in her, help her find her fire again.

She was a pretty girl, and his sister told him that boys called and sometimes came over. But she could take them or leave them, it seemed. Her first year of teaching, she hardly dated. She was busy with school. So, it was a big surprise when at Christmas, at the dinner table with just her and Mario and his sister there, Carol made the announcement that she was getting married.

"Where did you meet this man?" Mario asked.

"At school. His children are in my art class."

"He's divorced?"

"Yes, but he's very nice."

"What kind of work does he do?"

"Something to do with computers, marketing computers."

"He's a high class salesman."

A good smile on her face.

"He's quite a bit older than you?"

"Twelve years."

"Do you love this man?"

Now a big smile, but a very evasive answer: "Mario, you're the only man I've ever loved."

Mario looked at his sister. She said, "I think it's a good thing, Mario. She needs to have a home of her own, you know."

Yes. He knew. And maybe this marriage would finally bring her back to life. It could happen.

CHAPTER TWENTY

Taking a Risk, Part II

rigid was at the wheel. Captain Cushman, a protective arm around Mary, was in back urging Brigid, who needed no urging, to take the steeper faster ways across to the Club House. As the ride got rougher, Orion became giddy. In part she was excited to think she might run into Frank, but she was much more scared than excited. It would be something, though, for him to see her in her orange vest and with her hair wild and with these people, all misfits, really people like her, like she had been when she…when she felt like this before, when she jumped off the bridge at Echo Park Lake, when she kissed Dierdra. She glanced at Brigid. Brigid sees me. She hears me, too. It's all crazy, she told herself, but she felt like laughing or howling.

Orion glanced back to see how Mary was doing, but all

she saw was hair: Mary's, swirling round her head and her own slashing across her face and across her vision. Orion did laugh then at the mirror of her self she saw in Mary. She pointed to her head, and couldn't quite tell if Mary saw it, but she heard Mary laugh, and at the same moment, unexpectedly, there was Mary's hand in hers. Orion held her hair back with her arm and saw that Mary was now pointing to her own head and then to Orion's and she was laughing a surprisingly sane laugh: ordinary, like anyone's, no madness in it. And the feeling in her hand was so kind, so knowing, it completely sobered Orion. Then, just as suddenly, the hand was gone. And the laughter. The ride was over. They had arrived at the Club House.

"You two look like you were just electrocuted," Brigid said to the two women as they all climbed out of the Cushman.

The Captain rubbed his belly and rolled his eyes. "That comes after the crime."

Orion was last in line, just behind Brigid, Captain Cushman and Mary in the lead. Their orange vests were partially covered by their jackets, and no one seemed to be objecting to their being there, even though Mary had starting rearranging and organizing the candy bars on the counter.

To the right of the line sat the golfers. Orion kept her head down, studying the gouges made in the floor by cleated shoes. She listened to the golfers talk—bogies and eagles and irons and woods and what they should have used or done—but she didn't hear Frank's voice.

The air stank of stale beer, yet it triggered a craving in Orion. She could ask Captain Cushman to get her one, but somehow she didn't want to drink in front of Brigid. And what if he said no. There was something else in the air, something burnt, maybe coffee. Coffee would have to do.

She glanced up and saw that Mary had found a dishrag and was cleaning the counter and the brass rail and anything else within arm's reach. Neither Captain Cushman nor Brigid made a move to stop her, so Orion certainly wasn't going to. Anyway she knew it would just bring more attention their way.

Orion looked down again, trying to decide if she should chance a quick look at the golfers, just see if Frank was there. She turned her head toward the golfers, and as she did she felt the sweat break out on her forehead. The sweat scared her further, made her realize just how frightened she was, so all she saw in her confusion was the loud plaids and stripes of golf pants and the cleated shoes. Now she saw her sweat, one slow drop after another joining the pock marks on the floor. She wanted to wipe her brow, but she was afraid to. She looked more solidly down at the floor, and one big batch of her hair fell forward, shielding her from view. She stayed that way, feeling trapped, feeling ridiculous, wishing she could disappear.

"You can't just run away." For a moment Orion thought she'd spoken out loud, but it was Mary. Mary was next to Orion and she stamped her foot. "You hear? You can't just run away!" Orion was startled, shocked to hear Mary speak, shocked to be exposed, alarmed that Mary seemed to know her thoughts. She wasn't sure what Mary might do either. Brigid had turned and started to try to calm Mary down but she stopped when she saw that what Mary was saying meant something to Orion. Captain Cushman wasn't paying any attention—he was ordering chili dogs and coffee. "You can't do it!" Mary insisted.

One of the golfers got up, planted a smile on his face and went over to them. He addressed Brigid. "Something wrong here?" he asked.

It was Mary who answered him. "Yes," she said, "those pants you're wearing." Orion and Brigid held back their laughter, but looked at Mary with new appreciation.

"Say, are you supposed to be in here?" the golfer now addressed Frank who had returned to the group, arms laden.

"Just leaving, sir," he said as he ushered the women toward the door. "Have a nice day," he continued. "Great day for golf." They were at the door. He nodded toward the women, but was still talking to the golfer: "Hard to control your women these days." Then, just as they were going through the door, he winked and said: "Buy low, sell high." At last they were outside. Orion was laughing like a bad child, but Mary's words were ricocheting through her head.

A group of men had just parked their golf cart next to the Cushman, and as they got out, it seemed to Orion, it was hardly possible that they had ever fit into the tiny vehicle. They were so big, so tall, and they had their golf bags with them, as well. Orion watched as the men slung their bags, like quivers, over their backs. The clubs had little coverings on them, wool or flannel, some had fringe, all were brightly colored.

As the men approached, "Those pants" echoed in Orion's head and joined the rest of the chatter that was pressing against her temples and led her to study, through Mary's eyes, what the men were wearing. All four of them were wearing madras plaids of different color combinations, one different blues and purples, another reds and oranges and pinks, then greens, then browns. Their shirts, two of them, were striped and the other two were bright pink and kelly green with white Peter Pan collars. They had golfers' hats on, sort of tam o'shanters with pompoms in the center, but with the addition of flaps in the front to keep the sun out of their eyes—one might have had a flap on the back, too, maybe to keep the sun off his neck. The hats on the men and the little knitted coverings on their golf clubs that were bobbing up and down in the quivers over the men's shoulders struck Orion funny, and she thought she might laugh out loud, so she pulled her gaze down. But it did no good. The men's golf shoes looked too big, maybe because they were white and had so many tongues and flaps and tassels, and then the cleats made the men lift their feet higher than normal—they were not quite prancing, more like they were sneaking up on someone unaware of the noise they were making. All those fellows need, Orion said to herself, is fake noses. Then a laugh escaped her. She took a deep breath and looked up again at the golfers.

Everything changed. Walking toward her, in that foursome, was Frank, and, for just a second, she stopped, asking herself how it could have taken her so long to recognize her own husband. She moved and with the movement came an almost irresistible urge. It gripped her. She wanted to fall upon her knees and beg him for mercy, beg him not to see her. No. Beg him to see her. 'See me," she urged from within, as she managed to keep walking.

There couldn't have been more than ten feet of ground between her and Frank. He was talking to one of his friends, and that friend was looking at her, at the group, and he said something to Frank under his breath, a curling smile on his lips, and the other three men looked over at the group and laughed. Frank saw Orion. He had to. He looked straight at her. But then he said something, to the group, and the smile was now curled upon his lips as the other men laughed. Then, of a moment, they adjusted the look on their faces to something more innocent and good-natured, and they fixed their eyes straight ahead as they filed past Captain Cushman and Brigid and Mary and Orion.

"Did you see <u>those</u> pants? Brigid yelled at Orion.

"Indeed!" Orion heard herself say, and then louder, nearly screaming with laughter, "Indeed, I did."

Captain Cushman cocked his eye at Orion. "You in a mood to drive? We can cut along the firing range."

"Good idea," Orion said taking the wheel, and the four criminals drove off.

CHAPTER TWENTY-ONE

The Note, Part II

When she opened her eyes, the note was still in her hand. She placed it on the floor, leaving it under the table. She knew it wouldn't do any good to tell the man. He was powerless. And it wouldn't do any good to kill the housekeeper. She had to find out who wrote the note.

CHAPTER TWENTY-TWO

Filtered Light

Before she even opened her eyes, she knew someone was there, looking at her. Orion lay still for a moment, and then she sprang to her feet, crouched and ready to fight.

A man, dark and nearly naked, was standing across from her in the clearing. He held his hands up, as if to calm her. "Whoa," he said. "Wait a minute. This is my camp. My fire. You came to me."

It went through her head—not as words, but quicker and with certainty: I wrote the note! They held my hand, but I wrote the note!

Then she was fully conscious. She saw that it was just a man. This was his camp. She was in the mountains. Orion was relieved and a little embarrassed. She nearly giggled as she said, "I was having a very bad dream. The whole last year…." She had to control herself, control her laughter. "Sorry…I… lost

the trail." They both stood motionless, but she noted how fluid
and easy his stance was. The white lines in his face where the
sun hadn't penetrated told her he was ten or fifteen years older
than she. The lines were deep and looked like some sort of tat-
too or body adornment she'd seen somewhere before, in an art
book. Maybe it was a Maori he looked like. Maybe it was the
man she saw in her dream, the one in the boat.

The man smiled and made a slow deliberate turn, arms outstretched, like a hawk or an eagle, and when he faced her again,
Orion was embarrassed. "Excuse me for staring," she said, "but
there's something very familiar about you."

"I have the same feeling," he said. "Do you come here often?"

Orion knew it was a joke but she became even more embarrassed and, suddenly, very self-conscious. I must look like a mad
woman, she thought. Quickly she ran her hands through her
hair. It was knotted, matted, and from it she pulled a handful
of dust and leaves. She looked again at the man standing across
from her. His eyes had moved from her face to question the
blood, dried now, covering her arms and legs. Orion pointed,
laughter in her throat, down into the valley.

"I came through the Manzanita."

She saw his forehead clear. "Oh. Oh, well. You'll want to
wash those cuts. There's a creek just over that hill, behind that
old shack."

Orion looked up the hill and saw the shack. "What's it doing way up here in the wilderness?"

"What are you doing way up here in the wilderness?"

Orion was surprised by the question. Didn't know how to
answer. The man saw the confusion on Orion's face. He smiled,

kindly, and said, "It's probably an old miner's cabin. I use it for shelter if the weather gets too bad."

"You live up here?"

"Most of the time."

"Why?"

The man smiled, but didn't answer her.

"Why are you camped so far from the water?"

This time he thought for just a second and said, "So I can appreciate the water when I get to it."

Orion felt confused. Everything he said seemed to confuse or embarrass her, and she didn't know what to say to him.

"You maybe want to wash up. Those cuts could get infected. You'll need something warmer to wear." He reached into his backpack and pulled out a jacket and handed it to her. "There's some degradable soap in the pocket." Orion noted again how gracefully he moved. "The water in that creek's just above freezing—maybe a little warmer this late in the summer, and the sun gets cut off pretty early in the evening by those mountains to the west." He looked at the mountains and the position of the sun, then back to Orion. "It's getting close to seven, so you have a little while yet. You'll want to push off early in the morning. You'll pass the trail on the way up to the creek. Take it to your right, down the mountain. It'll take you all day."

"Do I have to boil the water before I drink it?"

"I drink it straight from the creek."

"Have you been sick?"

'Not from the water."

"From what?"

"Long story. What's your name?"

"Orion."

"Jack."

"Are you all right?"

"Yes. No. Yes, but… it's a long story too." She turned, uncertain, started to walk toward the creek, then, surprising herself, turned back and looked curiously at Jack, who had sensed
she wasn't through and stood waiting. In unexpected clarity of
mind and voice she said, "And to tell you the truth, I am sick
to death of it."

He smiled, nodded his head and then laughed. "That's very
funny. That's good. I'm sick of mine, too. Let's not tell each
other so we won't have to hear it again."

Now Orion laughed and she heard and felt that it was a
sane laugh, happy even. "Okay!" she said, as she turned again
and walked up the hill, saw the trail, passed the shed, and arrived at the creek. For the first time in months she felt light on
her feet. She felt she might be moving with some of the man's
energy, that he might have just sent some over to her as a gift.
He was generous, after all, she said, holding his jacket in her
arms. Going uphill she did not feel tired. She did not feel the
burden of her story.

But, my God she was parched. She threw the jacket over a
bush, quickly shed her boots and socks, stepped into a shallow
swath of water, squatted down and began cupping the water to
her mouth with her hand. But she couldn't get enough that way.
She stepped back up onto the bank, and tore her shorts and
shirt off. This time she felt the cold when her feet entered the
water. It was close to freezing, but she had to drink. She counted
to three and then dunked herself.

"Yeow!" she screamed when she surfaced. And then she
drank the water straight from the creek, no hands, like any

animal. Ah, it was satisfying, with a sweetness to it she had never tasted before. Really, she had never tasted water. Had not considered it when she drank it. Could only remember it as something she'd used to wash down aspirin.

Orion stayed there, dunking and drinking for a long time, and when, at last, she stood up and looked around her she felt good, and she saw that the water, the rocks, the earth were mottled with sunlight coming through the lodge pole pines. She looked down at her legs and arms, observing them as not exactly her, but as her body. The cuts weren't so bad, she thought, and she noticed her skin was mottled like the water and the rocks and the earth. So, beauty had been bestowed upon her, too. Almost immediately, and just for a split second, she had the feeling that she was someone else. She shook her head and stepped back onto the bank of the creek and then went to the place where she'd left the jacket.

As she went through the pockets, looking for the soap, she found a piece of paper, folded. She shouldn't look, she knew, but she did. It was a poem by someone named Rumi. Maybe that was Jack's last name. It was not a long poem. She read it quickly, but as she took in the meaning of the words, she found herself saying it out loud:

When a baby is taken from the wet nurse,
it easily forgets her
and starts eating solid food.
Seeds feed awhile on the ground
Then lift up into the sun.
So you should taste filtered light
and work your way toward a wisdom
that has no personal covering.

That's how you came here.
Like a star without a name,
Move across the night sky
with those anonymous lights.

If she didn't know better she'd have said that Jack planted the poem in his pocket for her to find—before…before, what? Before he knew I was alive? Orion shook her head.

She put the poem back in the jacket and found the soap. Then she returned to the creek, bathed, washed her hair, the cuts on her arms and legs. When she emerged from the creek, she felt very clean and sweet. Not Venus rising from the sea, she thought, but something like that. 'A creek god,' she smiled.

She found a flat sunny boulder to lie on, to warm and dry herself. Her body remembered the quarry at Santa Cruz, remembered Brigid, and a strong surge of energy ran through her. How powerful memory is, she thought, and lust, what a wonderful vital energy. Would she ever feel that again for another woman or for a man? It didn't seem to matter at the moment. The moment mattered. This being alive. "The girl," she remembered, "the girl deserves life." She recalled the gesture she made earlier, and patted her chest. "I am here," she said.

Ah, yes, she told herself, some grace has been granted at last. Grace and beauty. She turned onto her belly to look at the earth, at the soft banks of the creek, leafy at the water's edge, catching the sun, as it poured itself across the shaded rocks. It was that light again that she'd seen in thin bright lines on the black bags she'd filled with leaves at Pinecliff. She saw it in the patches of sunlit rocks, too. Sheaths of water ran over the bleached white rocks, the lines of water catching the sun widened into strings that she saw as sinew, and the water itself looked like a thin layer of skin covering the bony knees and shoulders of the rocks. And the music of the creek that she now, suddenly, became aware of was the sound of rattling bones and mysterious whispers. The sound touched her and awoke a memory that made her smile. So, she thought, there was beauty in Denise, too.

Orion turned again, this time to catch the color of the sky while there was still some light left in it. It pleased her to see that the moon had risen, barely visible in its frosty paleness, and that a few faint stars were there in the still daylight sky. The color of the sky eluded her. She couldn't name it. That pleased her, too. It was the color of twilight, she told herself, and those stars, they were the color of anonymous lights. She could join them if she understood the light.

And if she listened. She heard the sitar above the rattling creek. And she heard the pops and whirrs and sniggers of forest insects and forest animals. The trees sounded the soft whisk of a steel brush on a steel drum. She followed the lazy circles of the sound and fell into a reverie.

It was the cold night air that pulled her, reluctantly, back to the named world. Once she told herself that she was cold, she became much colder, and she shivered and jumped up, found her clothes and dressed. Her hands and chest were trembling with the cold as she put the man's jacket on. Oh, it was warm in that jacket, and she was grateful for it. She was grateful for this night, grateful for the anonymous lights, grateful.

She started back down the hill and saw the blaze of the campfire. She stopped. The tent was gone. So, he was gone. Her body tensed for a moment and then relaxed. Again her hand found her heart. I am here.

As she got closer to the fire she saw that he'd left a water flask and a nylon bag, probably food, hanging from a lodge pine. She thought to herself that she would hardly need it. She sat down near the fire, but it was the filtered light she felt, and she wanted nothing else.

The End

Made in the USA
Monee, IL
03 March 2022

92191803R00144